The Dodo Saga Volume 1

The Great Discovery

Author: Thomas Struchholz
Illustrations: Veronika Struchholz
Graphics: Rita Struchholz

Editor and publisher: Struchholz Kunst GbR, Veitshöchheim
Author and layout (InDesign CS 3): Thomas Struchholz
Illustrations (water colours and crayons): Veronika Struchholz
Graphics (Photoshop CS 3): Rita Struchholz

Printed by: Hinckel-Druck GmbH, Wertheim; www.hinckel.de
Printed on white opus praximatt, 115gr/m²
Font: Baskerville Old Face 11,8 pt
ISBN 978-3-9812318-2-3

© Struchholz Kunst GbR, Veitshöchheim, March 2010; www.struchholzkunstgbr.de

The copying and scanning of images and text from this book is strictly prohibited as too is the storage, modification and manipulation of data separately or with other material in PCs or other data carriers except with the prior written permission of the publisher. The publication of any part of this book, particularly in any digital media, is strictly prohibited, except with the prior written permission of the publisher.

Mix
Produktgruppe aus vorbildlich
bewirtschafteten Wäldern und anderen
kontrollierten Herkünften
www.fsc.org Zert.-Nr. SCS-COC-002594
© 1996 Forest Stewardship Council
FSC

Preface

Often little things lead quite by chance to something bigger. That is exactly how it was with this story. It all began with an article in the FAZ (A German newspaper). The article was about the dodo, a bird that has been extinct for 300 years. After reading the description of the birds, my elder daughter, Veronika, cried out in sympathy: "I'm a dodo!" Afterwards, she kept doodling funny human-like dodo sketches on paper. Shortly before Christmas 2007, these sketches inspired me to think up a short story to go with them. This was a special gift for my second younger daughter Regina. From just a few pages and a couple of quick sketches a manuscript emerged, which you, dear reader, now hold in your hands. After the whole family had enjoyed the story, we decided to take the plunge and risk the book, packed with imagination and humour, on a wider public. Our motto was: A long, long time ago, it may well have been the case that dodos really were clever birds ... Have fun!

Thomas Struchholz   Veitshöchheim, March 2010

Salient facts about the dodo:

The dodo
(Raphus cucullatus,
"hooded night bird")
was a flightless bird, about
a metre tall and lived solely on
the islands of Mauritius and Réunion
in the Indian Ocean. The dodo lived off
fermented fruits and nested on the ground. It
appears on the coat of arms of Mauritius.
Unfortunately, due to human stupidity and imported
predators, it died out at the end of the 17th century.

This information is based on an article about the dodo which appears in Wikipedia, the free online encyclopaedia, dated 19th March 2008, 17:38 UTC. URL: http://de.wikipedia.org/w/index.php?title=Dodo&oldid=43898491 (Downloaded on 19th March 2008, 19:44 UTC).

The Dodo Saga Volume 1
The Great Discovery

To
Regina

The Characters

Dodo Pushel
A dodo girl with a big appetite for fine food and adventure.

Gigi Pushel
Dodo's little sister. Dodo and Gigi adore each other — and get on each other's nerves.

Sine, the Mountain Elf
Sine´s role in life is to guard the purple crystal. Her laughter is magical.

Fuzz, Sine's fire-breathing dragon
Although still rather on the small side, Fuzz looks after Sine and her treasure. Unfortunately he sometimes forgets that he breathes fire.

Shmoncel Flattermann
Dodo's best friend. Shmoncel is a caterpillar who simply does not want to grow up.

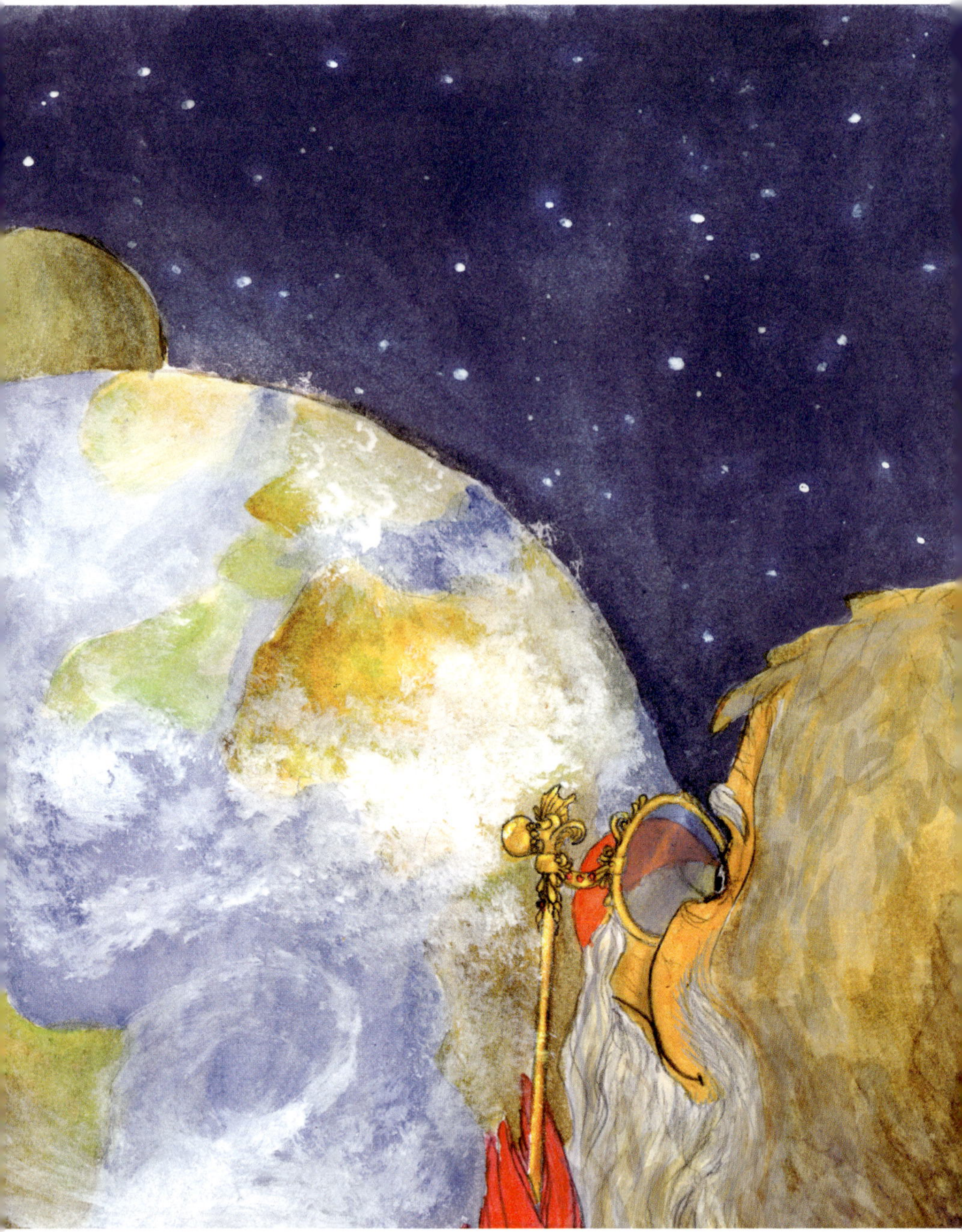

A long, long time ago on a continent far away, everybody lived together in peace and harmony. Life was wonderful. There was nothing to worry about. Well, perhaps we should say: Almost nothing.

The biggest worry was the weather. What it would be like the next day? Nothing annoyed the inhabitants more than bad weather. Nothing was dreaded more than a violent storm. However, on our paradise continent that only happened very rarely. Thank goodness! The scenery, in which our story unfolds, was like a beautiful dream: A wide, clear river opened out into the turquoise blue sea. A glorious and fine sandy beach lay off the coast where gentle waves rolled in day and night. The soothing rush of the surf mixed tirelessly with the voices and sounds of the wind, the birds, and all the other inhabitants of the island.

Along the river's long, exposed banks reeds intermingled with lilies, violets and brightly coloured irises and many other colourful and flourishing water plants. Quiet little lakes and ponds had formed secretly and furtively along the edge of the meandering banks. Beyond the landscape spilled over into open meadows that were full of flowers and orchids. Not far from here were the first trees and palms, which grew ever closer to each other as the land rose to the hills and mountains in the distance.

If you followed the rising terrain, you would wander through a great forest. The trees and bushes would grow ever more dense and glorious flowering shrubs would boldly pop through to entice insects. The face of the forest would change and new types of plants would cling to towering trees, some winding around the thick tree trunks, and others making themselves comfortable on the thick branches letting themselves hang lazily to the ground. Others hastened from their raised position to reach right up to the very treetops. They were simply taking advantage of the good nature of their larger relatives who majestically turned a blind eye to their impudence, choosing instead to wave their huge crowns back and forth in time with the wind.

Yet they appreciated and loved their lodgers with their resplendent colour and blossom. They were welcome ornaments. Finally you would arrive in the dense jungle with its overhanging ferns and magnificent orchids, with its free-swinging vines and cuddly-soft moss. Slender tentacle-like leaves eagerly reached out for the next morning dew or warm rain shower. The plants were so diverse and different at every floor of this magnificent greenhouse that whiling away a day here was always an experience. The myriad of voices and noises, the bewitching scents and smells in all their countless variations were almost unimaginable. They filled the floors and halls of this fantastic palace with pulsing life. The flowers and blossom competed daily for colour and fragrance.

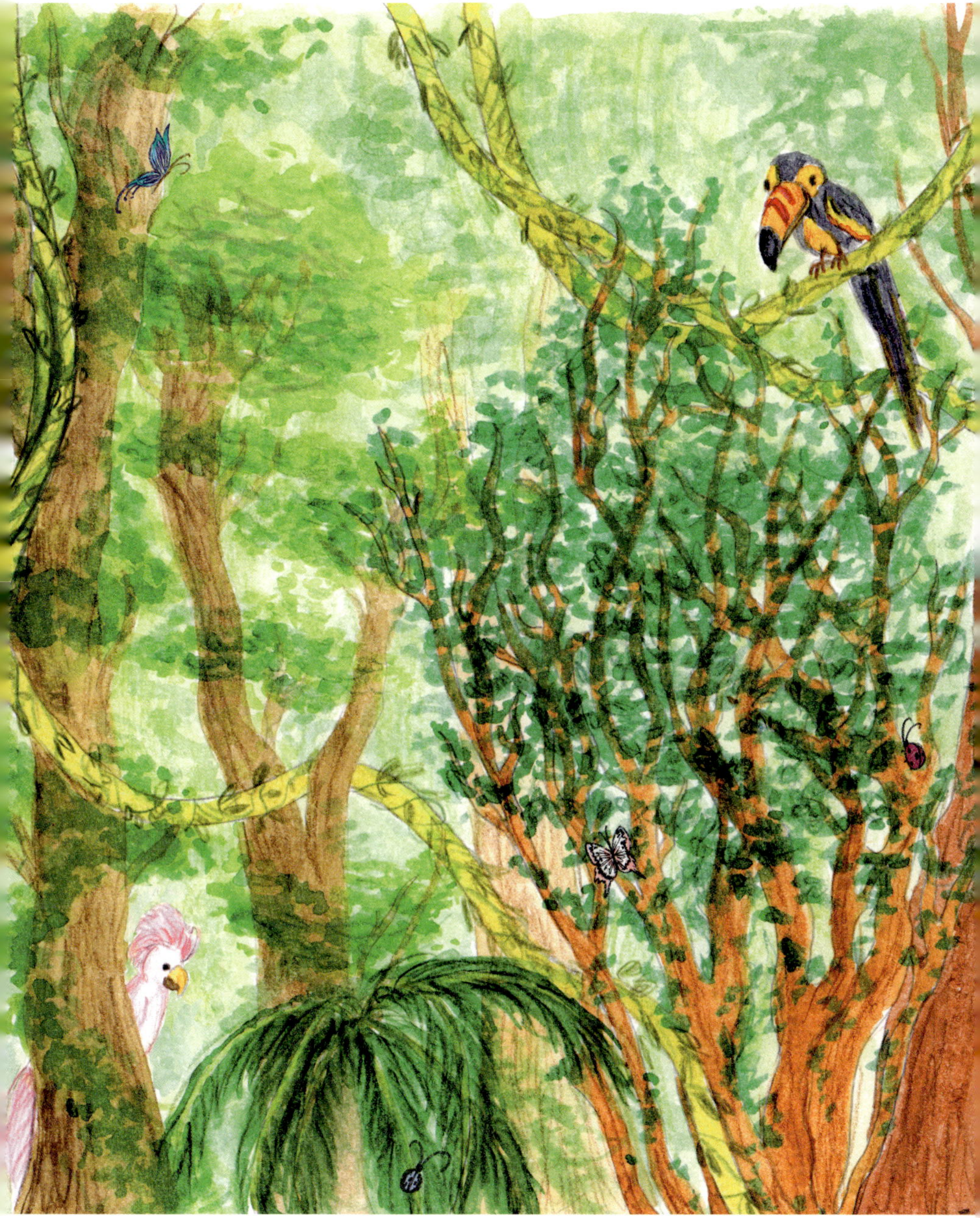

If the visitor only wanted to be at one with nature and was prepared to let his imagination run wild, he could stand and marvel at the breathtaking beauty of this wonderful far-flung paradise. Only then was it possible to take in all of the magic of this huge little world and truly experience it ...

To begin with, let us take a look at where the river opens up into the sea, and at the expanse of green meadows and the enchanting beach. Just a few steps away from the river was a large lawn with a prominent hill. On this very spot an impressive dodo colony had made a rather comfortable home for itself.

This hill was a really lovely spot. You could make a nice life for yourself here. The dodos had arranged their nests over the rambling hill. Some had built their nests close together. Others wanted a bit more space between themselves and their neighbours. It all depended on the preference of each family. The dodo hill had plenty of space. Time and again, a family would want to move and would seek out a new place to call home.

Such a move could be quite an ordeal if the whole family was involved in choosing a new spot with the entire nest in tow. The parents had their work cut out, especially if the children wanted to make a game of it. The children would take command of the move by pretending to be captains of a big ship. Poor old dodo daddy's beard feathers would sometimes stand on end. He had to bear the weight of the nest and keep his balance just because the little ones were playing a pirate game up there inside the nest.

The children found the rocking of the ship — um, I mean of course poor dad swaying around with the heavy home on his back — a most welcome diversion: "Rough seas! Pirates off starboard bow!" Such was the squawking that came out of the nest. The amiable new neighbour had to wonder whether this extremely friendly greeting was meant for him.

One lived for the moment. One could enjoy the wonderful weather almost the entire year — the only worry being, of course, that it might get worse the next day. Sometimes, a couple of fluffy white clouds on the horizon over the ocean could unsettle the whole colony of dodos for the rest of the day. There would simply be no other topic of conversation. Life could be no more beautiful in paradise.

Just on the edge of the hill was an ancient overgrown banana tree. At first glance, it looked like an impressive overhanging tree. Then, on closer inspection, you could see the large fruit-bearing bushes with glowing yellow fruit. You would then know what type of "tree" it was.

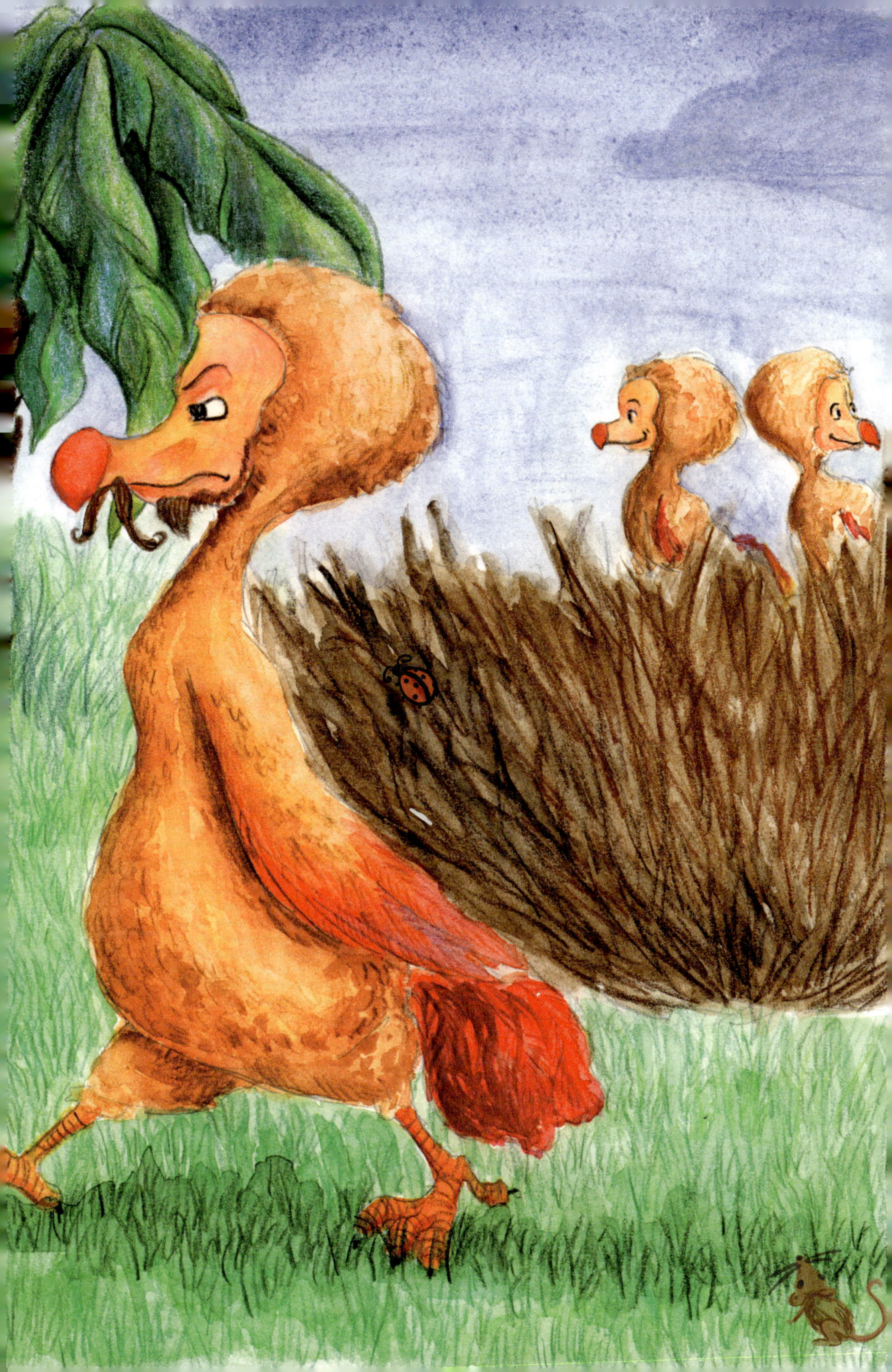

The Pushel family had made themselves at home underneath this massiv banana tree. Mum and Dad had two kids. The older was called Dodo, the younger Gigi. Whenever there was trouble in the Pushel household, you could be sure that Dodo and Gigi were behind it — and it sometimes led to loud protests all over the colony. Only recently, the two of them had got the whole colony in a dander by testing out their brazil nut catapult on the aforementioned banana tree. Even today, many dodos clutch various body parts, especially their heads, when they catch just a snippet of this story. I have no wish to recall how loud the protests of the entire dodo colony were on that particular day. That was quite something! What a disaster! The good-natured dodos were so outraged they even drowned out the roar of the ocean.

n other respects the Pushel family were very popular because they were so helpful. They had helped many a neighbour on many an occasion with their nest renovations. Papa was, after all, the best nest architect for miles around. His consultation services were much sought-after. He was very proud of his two children and generally took a good-humoured view of their pranks and crazy ideas. However, he drew a line when it came to the brazil nut catapult. This machine had given him a black eye, a green-pinkish lump on his forehead and a sore backside (which is still very sensitive today) — and only then was he able to bring the disastrous machine up on the banana tree to a standstill! But more about that another time ...

The average dodo in the colony lived a contemplative life enjoying each day to the full. Dodo and Gigi, however, had an appetite for adventure. There was always something to discover and they would think up such delightful pranks to play on their dear relatives. However, I shall tell you about that another time. I could write volumes on these pranks alone. One of their favourite hobbies was to dress up in very extravagant costumes. Dodo and Gigi were particularly fond of designing the most stunning dresses. They made these out of leaves, twigs, and fruit. They used fresh fruit makeup to paint their faces in bright colours or dyed various feathers in loud colours. This greatly alarmed their parents.

Papa was particularly embarrassed on one occasion when Dodo designed a large hat with oranges on top, dyed dark purple with aubergine peel, and painted her eyes, eyelashes, and cheeks beautifully to match. Poor Papa did not even recognise her, so Dodo was able to talk him out of three of the best specimens from his mussel collection by just fluttering her eyelashes.

Only when Gigi was no longer able to contain her laughter, and was rolling around on the ground behind the banana tree snorting and flapping her wings, did the light dawn on poor Papa. However, Dodo had already disappeared into thin air. She had bagged three of his best mussels! Boy, was the old man cross, all the more so because mum too was laughing heartily at his expense. She took every opportunity to flutter her eyes at him over the next few days!

Dodo's best friend was Shmoncel. He was a caterpillar. He was as long as your arm. He had a big round head, on top of which two long feelers hung forwards in a wide arc. On either side he had two other coiled feelers with shiny black balls on their tips which wobbled about when he was excited.

Shmoncel's skin shimmered light green like the finest silk. It was decorated with white, red, and blue stripes along its entire length. The tiny hairs on his body glittered in the most beautiful colours of the rainbow. At the end of his back sat a large, luminous, curved horn which he proudly carried around like a lantern. Shmoncel simply was in no hurry to become a butterfly. Life as a caterpillar, with Dodo for company, was much more to his liking. That certainly had something to do with the fact that, for most of the time, Dodo carried "her" Shmoncel around on her back. The reason for this was that his short legs were not quick enough to keep up with her. The two were simply inseparable. In actual fact, Shmoncel was the little brother in the dodo family.

The three of them had already had some feather-ruffling adventures. They often sat right up in the canopy of the banana tree. It was like a robbers' den. There they would think up new pranks and adventures — and it usually did not take them too long to put these into effect.

Gigi would often kick up a fuss because she was not allowed to go everywhere with her big sister. She would then sit defiantly up in the banana tree. From up there she would follow the course of the action — that is to say what the other two got up to — with military precision.

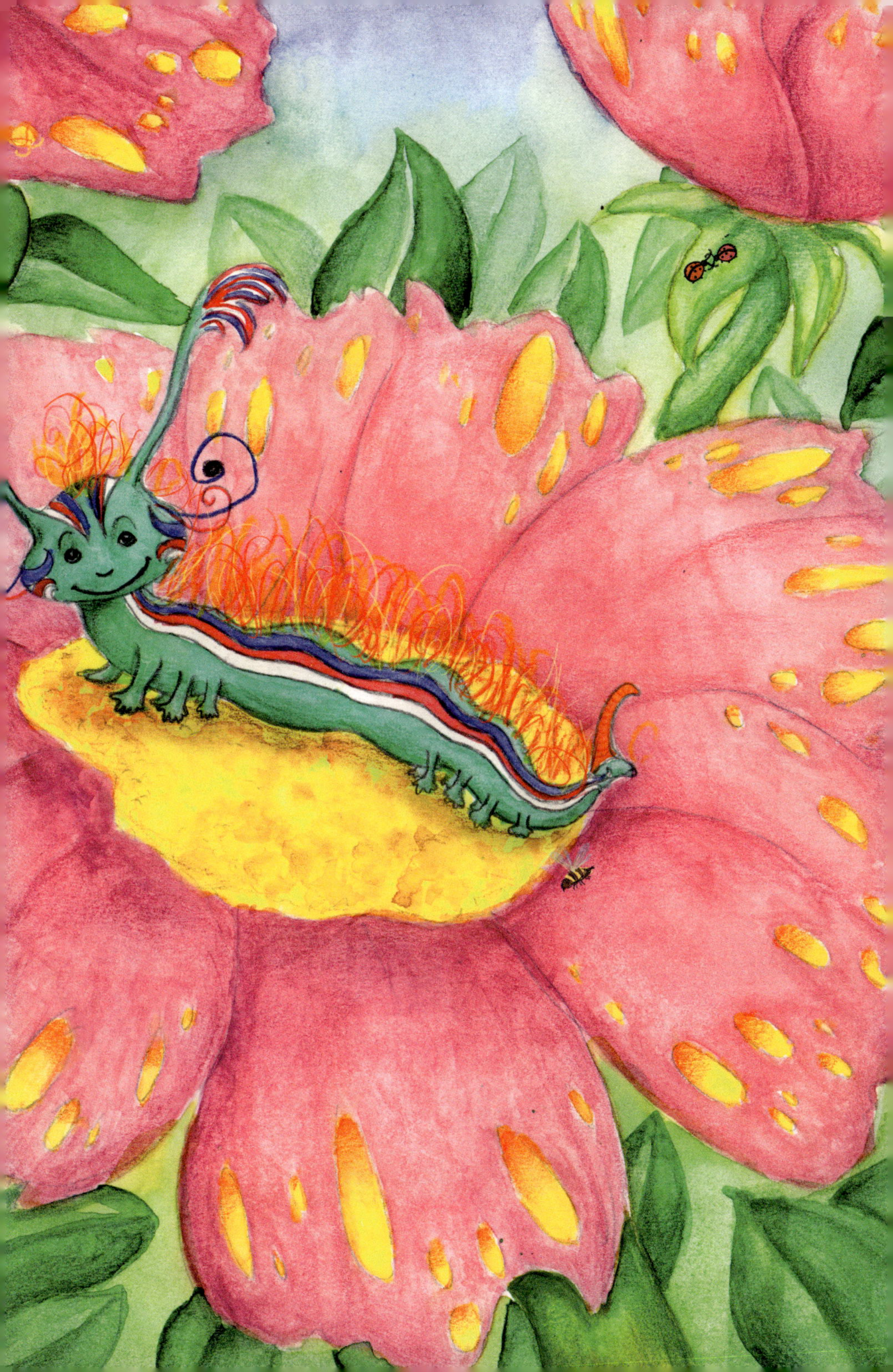

What a lot of cackling and screeching there was if **Gigi** happened to lose sight of the two. The whole banana tree would then tremble while **Gigi** performed her wild dance up in the treetop. **Mama** and **Papa** would sometimes be at the receiving end of the odd overripe banana, which certainly amused the neighbours who chuckled and chortled by way of acknowledgement.

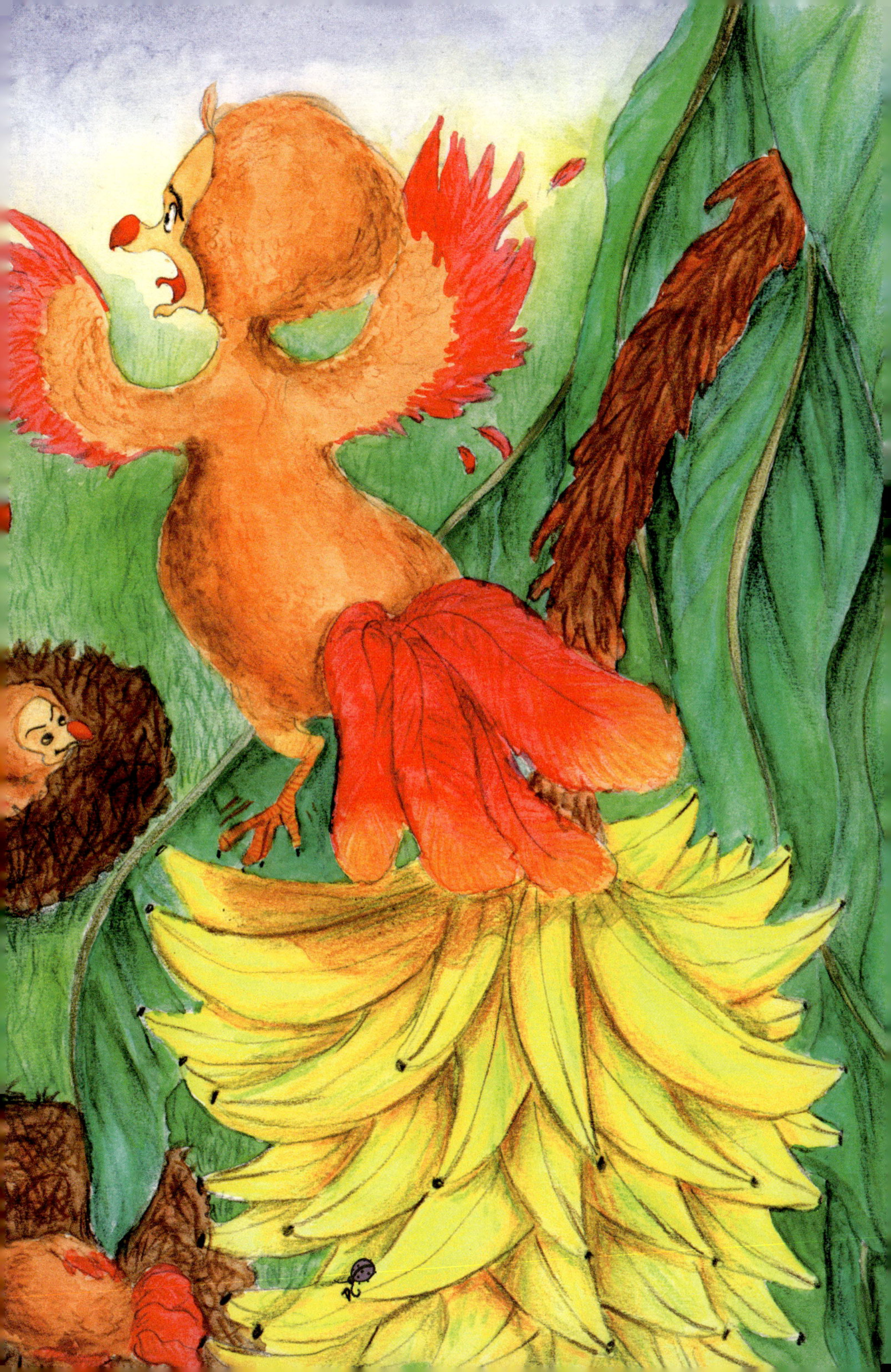

Then Mama would cogitate on whether to put banana granola on the dinner menu yet again that evening or whether to spare herself the moans and groans from Gigi and Papa. Neither of them understood the true value of banana granola. Meanwhile, Papa would bellow up to Gigi, giving her a good dressing-down. However, Gigi never seemed particularly bothered, much to her father's annoyance. She knew only too well that he would not expend the effort of climbing up the banana tree. Usually, she just stayed quiet and waited until things had settled down below. Mama and Papa looked up and gave each other a wink: "Same temperament as your mother. Unmistakable, my dear!" When Papa let slip this remark, Mama would always respond: "Well, actually, your wild father comes to mind, the one they called 'Cowboy Puschel'! Don't you think, dear?" The conversation usually fizzled out with them sticking their tongues out at each other or with Gigi performing another banana dance, for whatever reason.

One night a heavy storm blew in off the ocean. The deep roll of thunder mixed menacingly with the foaming surf of the normally peaceful blue-green sea. The small waves of the previous day had overnight become large breakers that slammed onto the sandy beach. There were blinding flashes of lightning throughout the night. The dodos thought they could see spirits and spectres, ghosts and ghouls riding on the whitecaps, with the howling wind whipping the water into wild vortexes in the air.

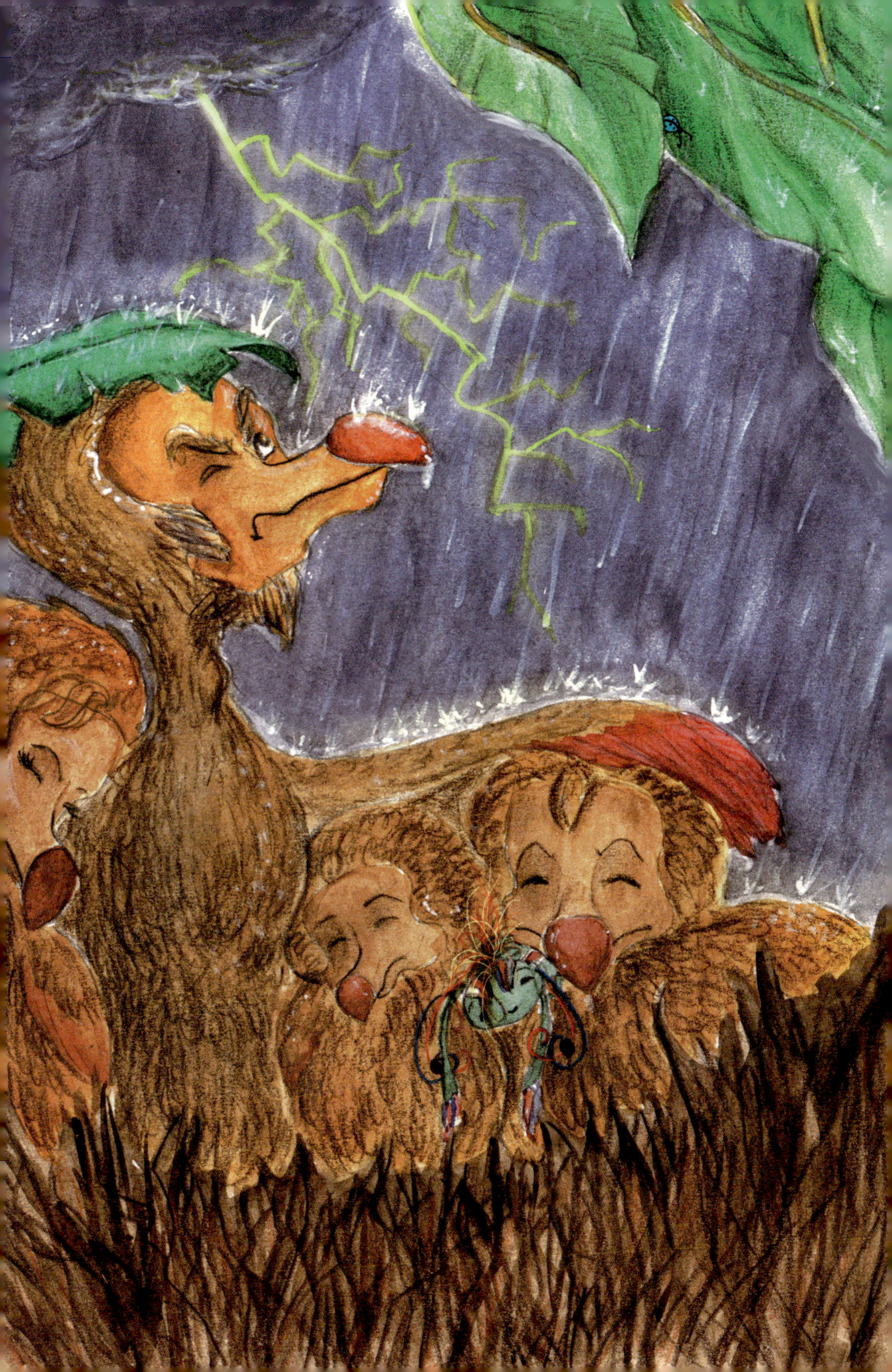

There was no mistake. What had to happen, happened. The weather really did take a turn for the worse. Everybody knew it was coming, but nobody paid the slightest attention. The weather had paid no attention at all. It paid attention to no one. All the dodos sat huddled together in their nests, heads pulled in close to their bodies, hoping for some improvement in the weather. Yet this time the weather had no compassion for our poor dodos. It really did want to go on the rampage and show who was the real boss on the island. The storm raged all night long. The wind howled through the banana tree and threatened to uproot it. Papa kept one eye open and squinted up. He fumed at each fat raindrop that landed right in his eye. "Right, that's it," he vowed. "Tomorrow, we're upping sticks. We're moving ... " Everyone was very glum as they hunkered down in their nest. Nobody really wanted to listen to him. Everyone hoped that the weather would finally decide to get better.

The entire dodo colony protested loudly at each flash of lightning, but the rattling rain and whistling wind quickly drowned out their cries. It was a long wait through the dark night, and hardly anyone could think of getting any sleep. Only towards morning did the wind begin to subside, so that the rain came down in torrents. The dodos were utterly exhausted. Finally they got some peace and slowly sank into a deep sleep.

As dawn broke, a light blue strip appeared on the horizon. It got wider and wider until the sun burst out over the sea streaming its golden rays. Slowly the sea grew still. It looked as if the warm sunbeams were stroking the water and smoothing out the waves. Yet most of the residents slept through this wonderful sunrise or just dozed lazily right in front of it.

Slowly the dodos awoke from their slumber. They shot angry looks at the retreating clouds and fluffed up their wet feathers to let the warm sunshine in.

As Dodo and Shmoncel awoke and the sun winked at them over the edge of the nest, they noticed at once that the day's fresh morning breeze had a particularly fragrant and exciting aroma. They stretched. Dodo and Gigi sat on the edge of the nest fluffing up their feathers to their hearts' content. "Good morning Mama, good morning Papa!" they chirped in unison balancing on the edge of the nest.

Dodo and Shmoncel liked this morning of all mornings. There was something quite different about it. However, little did they know that this morning would mark the beginning of an extremely exciting but utterly exhausting day. Bursting for action, they hurried down their breakfast. They could not wait to get going. Alas, once again Papa did not let little Gigi accompany Dodo and Shmoncel into the forest. After much moaning and groaning, Gigi took up her lookout position.

The sun transformed the rainforest into a glittering palace of diamonds and gems with, dare I say, every colour under the sun. Raindrops glittered all around on the orchids, on the delicate leaves of the ferns, and on the tips of the leaves on the trees. Dodo chuckled with joy every time these raindrops coalesced to cascade from the petals down onto the ground.

The sun's rays broke into the myriad drops of water to form a colourful display of sparkling and shining fireworks that shot off in every colour of the rainbow. Dodo and Shmoncel were entranced. These colours were a feast for the eyes! Do you think that we should be going so far from home?" remarked Shmoncel tearing Dodo out of her dreams. As she took in the blaze of colour, Dodo gazed around in amazement. "Oh," was all that she could say. They had indeed crossed the big wide meadows, to the trees, bushes, blossom. They were now deep in the forest, on the path leading up the mountain. They must have been walking for more than two hours. "Come on!" mumbled Dodo. "What could happen? Now that we're here let's go up to the plateau where we will be able to see the sea!"

Shmoncel responded somewhat meekly: "Then we should have let our parents know, don't you think?" "What? Run back home now and then come all the way back here again? They wouldn't stand for it. I wouldn't be able to manage it either. Let's just carry on. Gigi saw which way we went. She would definitely have told Mama and Papa. That means your parents will know too." "Well, if you say so," agreed Shmoncel, rocking his head thoughtfully to and fro. His two big feelers wobbled, shedding the last drops of rain. "Then we'll have to get a move on!"

"**H**a! What you mean to say is: I should get a move on," said Dodo. "It's my feet that are carrying us both! Anyway, let's hit the road," she commanded energetically. "Since we've got this far, we should really make it worth our while!" Dodo set off striding out with Shmoncel on her back. Before long, however, she was huffing and puffing. The path kept snaking uphill. They had to cross small streams, and next to the trail they could see the little runnels that rushed the water down into the valley.

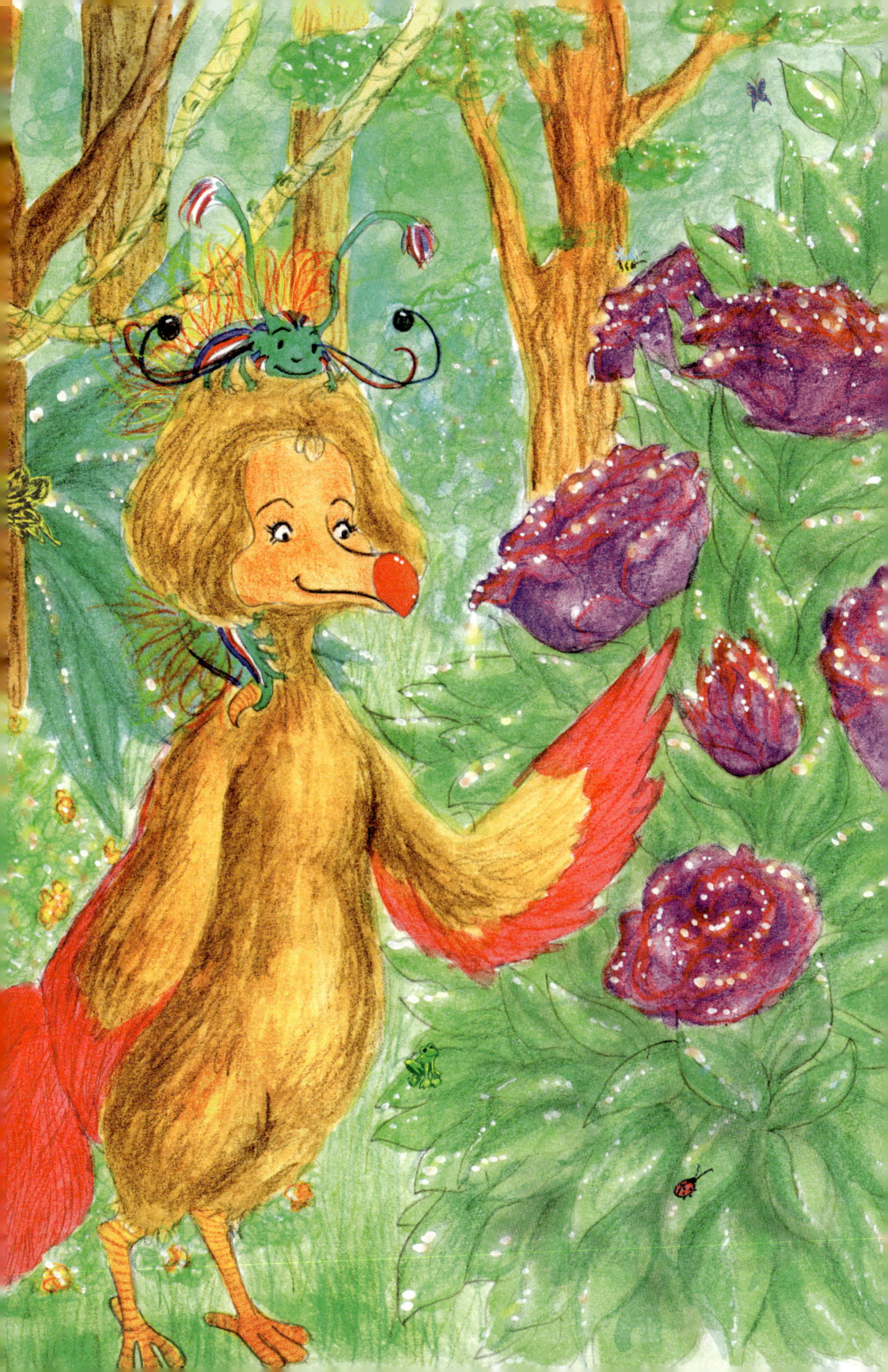

They walked for a long time pushing deeper and deeper into the forest. The easy forest trail had narrowed to a dirt track, which was used just often enough not to be completely overgrown. Little by little the two struggled uphill along the track. Forest turned into jungle. Untouched nature surrounded them. Their gaze no longer shot into the distance, but stuck to the ground or turned up to the mighty treetops. Shmoncel tried to help Dodo by fending off leaves and twigs. They struggled on together. They had become very quiet. Loud and strange noises pressed in on them, breaking into a bewildering cacophony of echoes under the forest roof. The moist, warm air had started to affect Dodo. She secretly asked herself whether she had made the right decision or if her courage had turned into foolhardy recklessness. "If the weather gets bad now, we'll be in a right pickle," she murmured quietly to herself. Shmoncel thought he heard Dodo say something about 'pickled mangoes'. "What do you mean 'pickled mangoes'? Down here, I can see nothing but different shades of green, but not one piece of 'pickled mango'. Why should I care pickled mangoes? Are you hungry again? You never stop picking berries and then you wonder why it's getting more difficult ... "

Astonishing! It was very rare for Shmoncel to be so grumpy and bad-tempered with his best friend. The fear of being in the wrong place and of biting off more than he could chew tormented him. Would it not have been better to have discouraged his friend from embarking on this adventure?

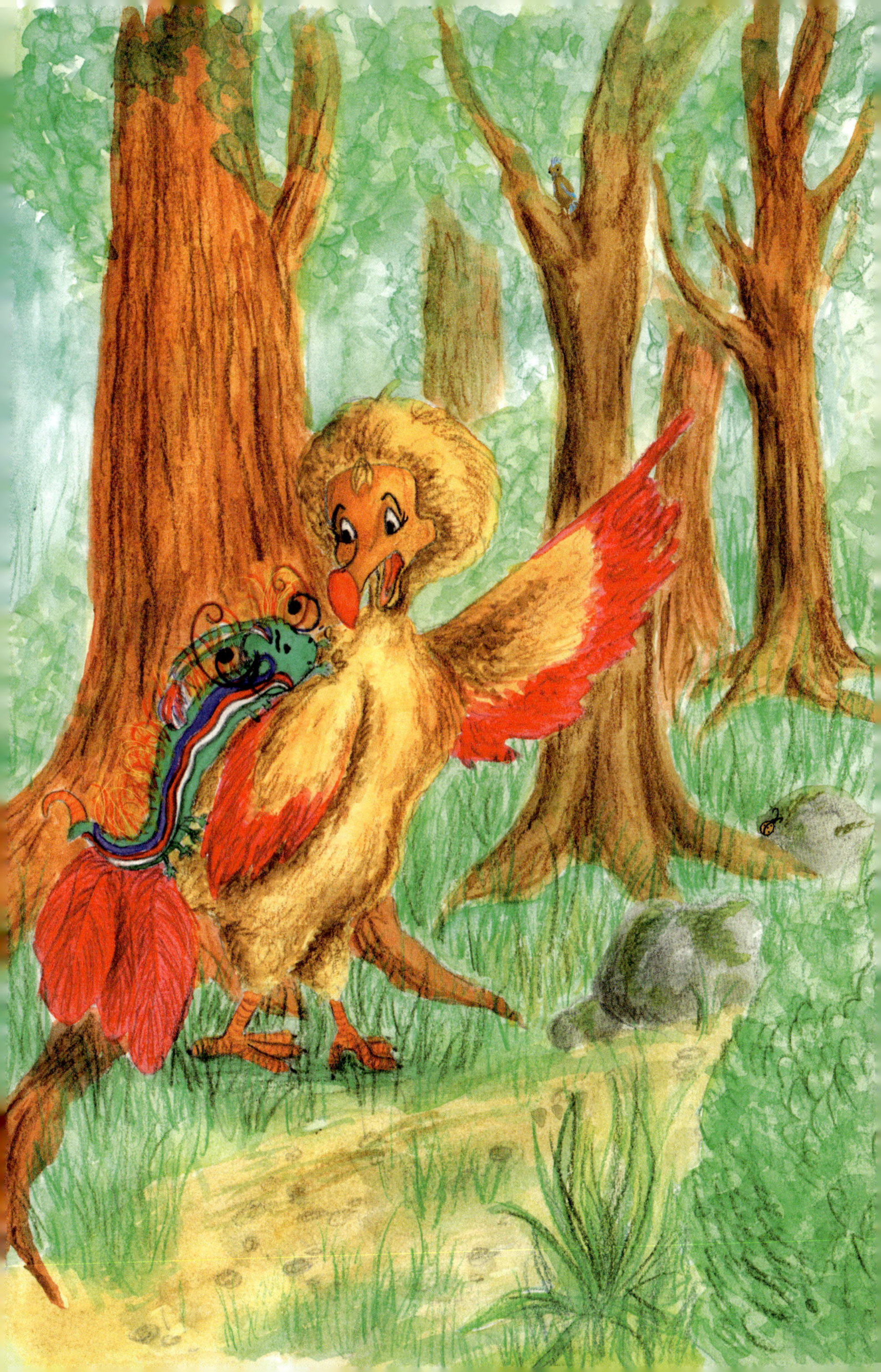

"Yes, my dear. Are you trying to suggest that I eat too much?" grumbled Dodo. "No, no! I just didn't understand what pickled mangoes has got to do with all this and that's why ... " "Yeah, right," interrupted Dodo abruptly. "I'm walking my socks off and you're making silly remarks. As if I said anything about food!" She snapped, hissing the words through her half-closed beak.

"For your information, I've been worrying about the weather. It's getting darker and darker here and I'm longing for a bit of blue sky. Forget about the food. Mind you, I could really do with a break and a good lunch. I'm as hungry as a bear." "But you've been eating non-stop, while ... " Shmoncel chose not to complete the sentence as deep angry frown lines appeared on Dodo's forehead. Dodo looked at him and squawked: "You're not starting again, are you?"

Shmoncel's feelers at once began to wobble about in a frightful manner and he quickly steered the conversation to another topic. "Look straight ahead. It's getting a lot brighter. We must be getting out of this thick jungle soon." Shmoncel looked ahead. Then overjoyed — and to his great relief — he declared: "Dodo, you're great! You actually did it!" He was standing up to his full height on Dodo's back, supporting himself using her beak and head. He was right in front of her eyes leaving her to squint at his belly.

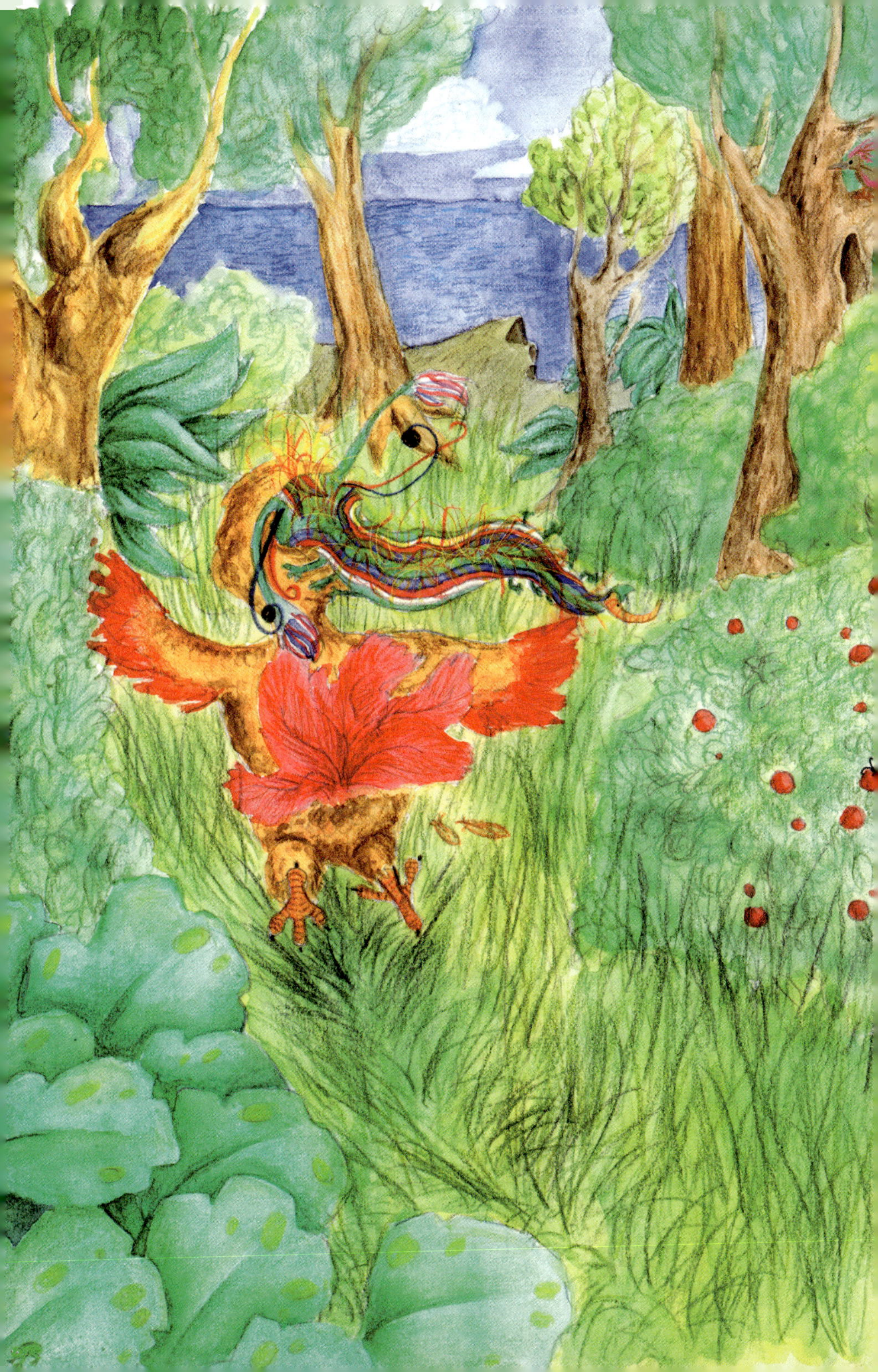

He looked forward, his eyes beaming. "Would you be so kind as to let me turn my head so that I can actually see something, too?!" mumbled Dodo into his belly. She then slowly turned her head so that Shmoncel would not fall off. "Of course, but look straight ahead of you ... " Shmoncel was really excited. He was so excited that he was groping around on Dodos face. She peeked through his little hands. Finally she could see for herself.

"Cool!" Dodo blurted. She turned her eyes onto full beam and began to run. Yes, she literally sprinted down the path which was virtually overgrown. "Ouch, ahhh! ... " shrieked Dodo. "Would you kindly take your paws out of my peepers!" trumpeted Dodo, shaking her head indignantly. Shmoncel would have gone flying had he not grabbed on to everything within reach of his hands and feet. Now Dodo could see nothing out of her left eye because Shmoncel's little hands were holding tight onto one of her eyelids. He had pulled it down to half mast. "Kindly let go! Otherwise, I'll go into a skid and we'll end up somewhere in a tree. Besides — it hurts!" "Sorry, sorry!" apologised Shmoncel trying to sit back down normally. Huffing and puffing, Dodo scampered on. Her energy was sapping. She simply could not run any more. After a short while, they came to a sort of clearing, which sloped gently uphill. There were a few trees surrounded by high grass. "Why does the jungle end here so abruptly?" asked Dodo with genuine wonder.

Shmoncel answered: "My mum told me once that the plateau was created during a storm. The lightning struck a mighty tree, a fire broke out and a huge hole was burned into the jungle. She barely made it out alive. Luckily, the fire was put out by the heavy rain that started just after the lightning struck. Ever since then, there's been this plateau." "Hmm" was all that Dodo could say with the little breath she had left. "I've always said that there should be a ban on bad weather. It'll just end in a real climate catastrophe ... Just you see ... pffft ... pffft ... ! When I think about last night, the whole night ... pffft ... just don't think about it ... pffft ... pfft ... suppose we had had that lousy weather today! ... pffft! ... And no Mama and Papa! I would have dropped dead! ... pffft ... Pretty careless, what we've done ... " Shmoncel nodded slowly in time with his feelers, but chose not to say anything. After all, he had been feeling uneasy about it in the meadows down in the valley. They had never been so far away from home by themselves. But the wonderful view quickly dispelled their worries.

No exaggeration, the sight that greeted them was like a dream. They had a fabulous view of the sea. They could see the small bay near their home and the mouth of the river, which from their vantage point looked like a silver-blue ribbon snaking through the meadows to the coast. Further inland, they could make out the dodo colony, and they could even see the banana tree! Were it not for the fact that it was so far away, Dodo could have sworn that she could see Gigi sitting at the top! "Man, isn't that gorgeous!" gushed Dodo. "Man, isn't that gorgeous," echoed Shmoncel from her back looking as if he wanted to stretch out further. He shamelessly took advantage of Dodo's patience by balancing right on top of her head, with two hands under her chin and two hands clasped right over her eyebrows. Now, whenever Dodo turned her head, he simply turned with her, like a periscope. All he had to now was bark out orders about where to look. He sighed. "I could stay here for hours. Such a wonderful view. Not even our banana tree comes close, not by a long stretch. By the way, was that your stomach I heared rumbling? Hey Look! Over there's a ripe mango that's got our names on it." Dodo had no compunction when it came to food. Food was incredibly important to her. It certainly came a close second to family and friends. However, the current reading in her stomach strongly influenced that ranking. She turned her head with lightning speed so that Shmoncel's top half went flying and he would have fallen had it not been for all his other little hands and feet clinging on tightly. "Mango!?! Where?! Ah-ha!" And on that note, the view momentarily paled into insignificance.

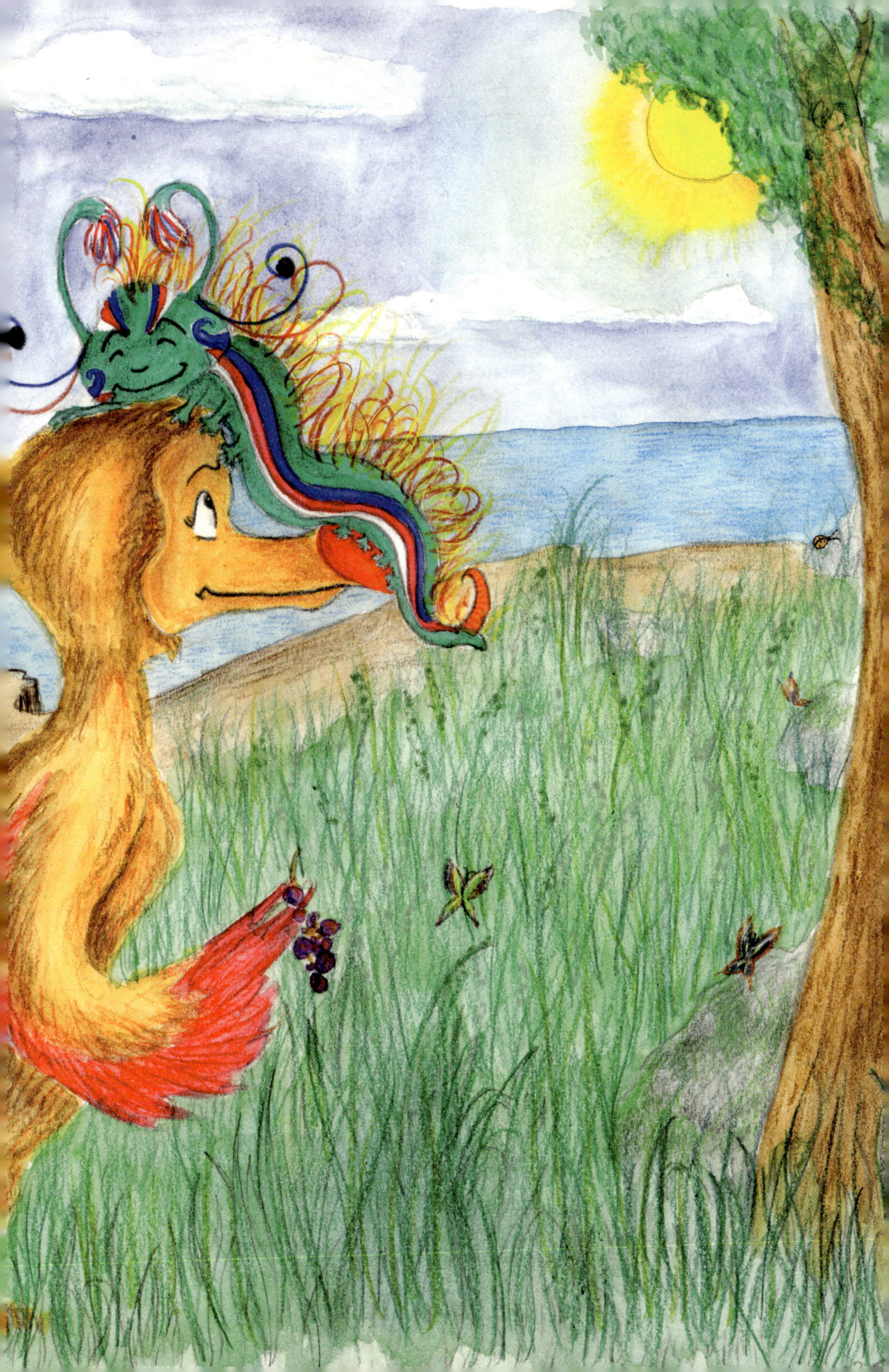

"Oh, yeah!" were the only words that escaped from Dodo's mouth. She leapt like a long jumper up the mango tree. SLURP — was all that Shmoncel heard — and then the whole mango was in her beak. "HEY, I said that it had OUR names on it!" cried Shmoncel. "Ohmm, mexcmuseme myi maametemy murmot," was all she could manage. This was something along the lines of: I totally forgot about that. However, not far away the next mango was ready for picking. Shmoncel could get his money's worth too. He savoured every little morsel, he enjoyed every little bit. Dodo, on the other hand, had just taken another great mouthful. The half that she had offered Shmoncel out of friendship was gone again. Dodo quickly explained, "I think half should be enough for you, so you don't get a stomach ache, right?" Shmoncel just rolled his eyes, kept his own counsel, and took care not to get any mango on Dodo's beautiful feathers. He inspected the fine feathers on her neck and back, and determined that she would have to give her plumage a thoroughly good clean when they got home because he had really flattened them by riding around on her back all day. He would have to help her. It was an arduous and time-consuming chore which Dodo loathed, especially after a nice day of playing.

Dodo had a guilty conscience. "Should I get you another mango?" she asked. "Are you full from just that half? I won't take any more from you. Are you angry with me now? You offered me a half! Didn't you?"

"It's o.k.," he reassured his best friend. He knew Dodo ate well to live well. Eating was her favourite pastime. There was no holding her back when it came to sweet and juicy fruit. Whenever the colony had a party celebration and laid on a beautiful fruit buffet, Dodo sometimes had to be physically restrained. Otherwise, she would probably sit down in the middle and defend her bounty like a lion. Shmoncel was the only one who was allowed to come near her. Mean gossip suggested that this was only because he ate so slowly and could not possibly eat everything out from under her. But, that's just nonsense of course ...

"Let's just walk a little bit further today," suggested Dodo, who was obviously back to full strength after the vitamin-rich refreshment. "No, I don't want to," said Shmoncel. "Oh come on, just a few more steps! Look, just as far as that ledge up there where the cliff peeks out." Dodo was trying to win him over. Between two high palm trees stood a majestic red sandstone cliff that was at least three times the height of their big banana tree. Cliffs like this one were rare. It had a face. It looked as if a jaguar had settled down there to peer out over his domain. The two palm trees to the left and right of the face looked very amusing. They looked like the ears of a jaguar! A red-brown jaguar with green ears!

"Alright then, but no further than that!" relented Shmoncel squinting up and trying to figure out the position of the sun. They had to be home by tonight, at any rate. "We can definitely enjoy the view better up there," determined Dodo. She began to run. Arriving at the cliff, Dodo had to pick her way carefully up the terrain at the side in order to reach the top. "Thank goodness the jaguar's bald," remarked Shmoncel. "Otherwise, all this work wouldn't be worth it!" "Work is good. You're a fine one to talk! You've got rather heavy after this long climb. I can feel my back all the way down to my tail feathers!" Dodo had found it difficult and demanding to climb up through the bushes to the top of the cliff. "I wouldn't mind a sip of water right now," she cawed. It was very dry here on the cliff.

There was almost nothing here except for rock, the two palm trees, and the thick bushes to the side of the jaguar head — and there was not a single piece of juicy fruit to be found there.

"Holy hoppin' mango! That's a real mess of thorns. Looks as if someone up there doesn't want any visitors. There's not even a dirt path," panted Dodo using her beak and wings to pave her way through it. "Do you think we'll run into any trouble up there? Wouldn't it be better if we just leave?" came the somewhat helpless suggestion from Dodo's back. What could Shmoncel do? Running and walking weren't his strong points. Everybody knew that. "Not now, I'm almost there. Look ... " Dodo had actually fought her way through again. One more leap and they were on the rocky plateau. It had almost no plants or grass growing on it, bar a few thorny bushes in little crevices and a few orchids which stood out with large purple blossom dangling at the end of their long stems. The blossom itself hung like open sacks and swayed gently in the light breeze that blew up over the cliff from the sea.

They looked around. The view that greeted them was even more stunning than before. The panorama was spectacular. From here, the eye swept across the island, the forests and the blue sea. They searched for their home which now looked even smaller than before, but they could still make it out. The banana tree was clearly visible on the hill. Their eyes glazed over and Dodo's beak fell open in awe! Such a view was completely unexpected.

Dodo was almost spent of energy, yet she was so excited that she hopped up and down, waving down at the banana tree, yelling: "GIGIII, GIGIIIII, here I am. GIGI!" — as if Gigi could see and hear her. On her back, Shmoncel seesawed his head in the opposite direction. His feelers looked wildly out of control and had almost tied themselves in knots. He stammered, "Stop it! All your hopping and bopping is making me ill! I'm not a kangaroo. Stop right now! Otherwise, you'll have digested mango all over your back."

Dodo turned her head. "Oops," she said grinning at Shmoncel. He rolled his eyes and the corners of his caterpillar mouth drooped ominously. Finally out it came: "Buuuurp". He quickly put his little caterpillar hands to his mouth. "Pardon me," he mumbled, "but putting up with all that back-hopping takes its toll. Next time, let me down first before you go crazy like that and mutate into a kangaroo. Buuurrrppp ... Pardon me!"

Our two friends enjoyed the marvellous view for quite a while. Dodo's eyes then swept over the terrain behind her. It was a rocky landscape that climbed up and up beyond the cliff where the bushes grew more sparsely. "Look at that!" they exclaimed. The foot of the rocks was completely overgrown by a large thorny bush. "Behind that bush is the entrance to a cave," said Dodo. Shmoncel agreed. "I can see it too. Let's take a closer look."

Moments later, they were standing right in front of the bush. They could now see the entrance to the cave. It was well concealed. The thorny bush had almost completely grown over it. There was an abundance of tiny crimson flowers on its branches — and no leaves — and they could therefore dimly discern the dark shadow in the background. The flowers themselves looked like small drops of blood and glowed a rich, vivid red.

"I could probably crawl in there," muttered Shmoncel, "but I'm not too crazy about these thorns." "Well, we can take care of that," reckoned Dodo. She began to hack away at the branches with her sturdy beak. The flowers gave off a wonderfully sweet smell which Dodo thought would taste of honey. Shmoncel would have liked to have tried it, but with all the thorns and twigs flying, he thought it advisable just to hold on tight and keep his head in.

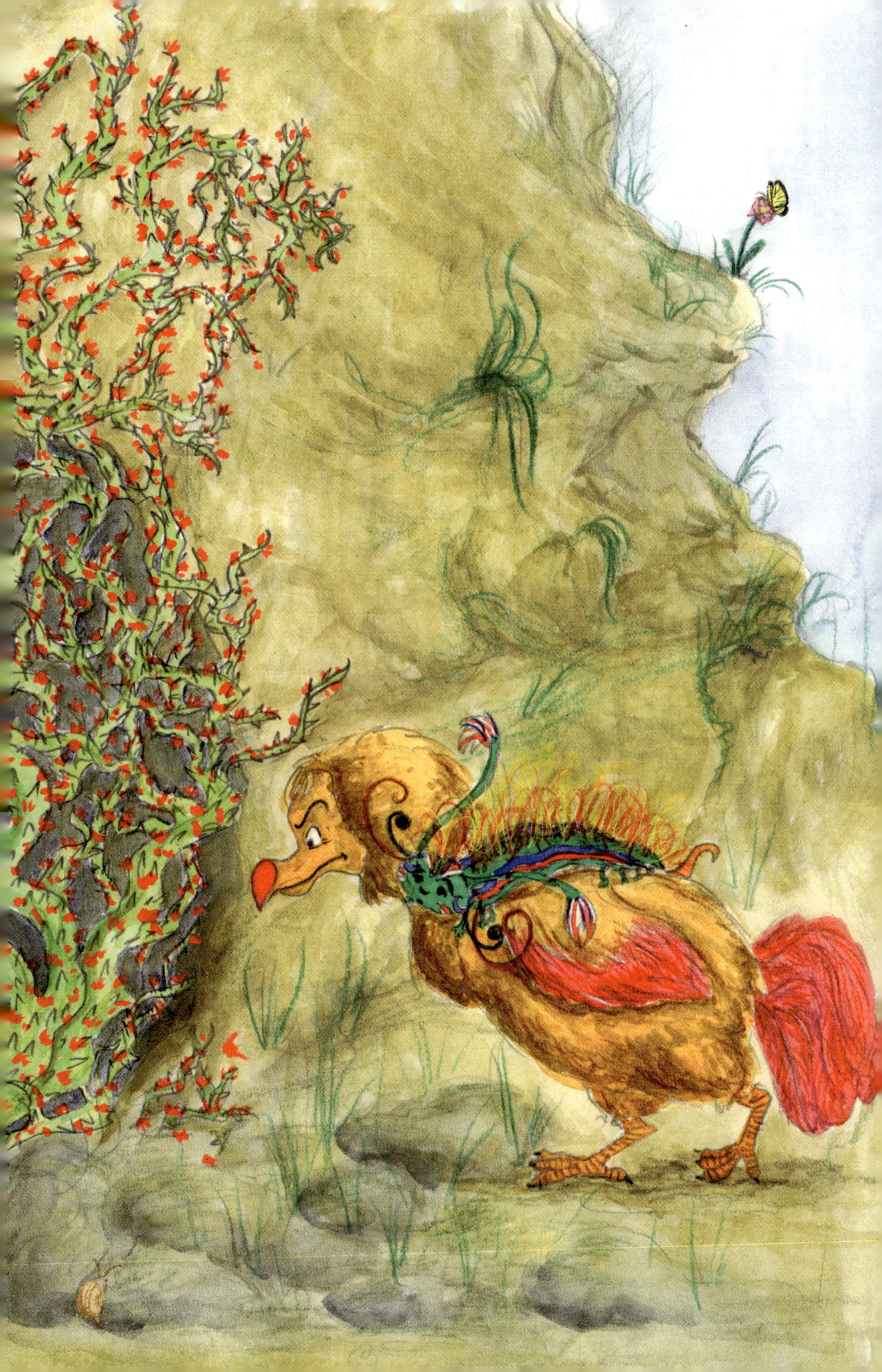

Dodo was sending a dangerous storm of brush into the air, to the left and right of him, and he did not want to catch anything on his ear, or rather, his feelers. Just a few minutes later, Dodo had actually managed to knock out a sizeable hole in the mess of thorns which they might be able to crawl through into the cave. "Watch out!" cried Shmoncel, "I don't want to get skewered!" — at which point he crawled under Dodo's beautiful feather coat until only half his head and his two wobbling feelers were protruding. His voice was now very muffled. "This weird bush has taken over the path too."

No sooner had Shmoncel finished his sentence than Dodo stopped abruptly and broke into a giggle. Her little wings suddenly started revolving and she performed a wild tap dance, hopping from one leg to the other. "Stop it right now!" she giggled and snorted, "I'm dyyyiiinnngg." Shmoncel clung on for dear life. He thought she was coming down with cave fever. "She had better stop her hopping right now. It's making me dizzy, and if she carries on I'm going to get really sick," thought Shmoncel. His feelers and eyes flounced up and down. This did not do him any good at all. The corners of his mouth drooped ominously. "Stop tickling, right now ... !" yelped Dodo, madly scratching herself on the ground and laughing with an open beak as if possessed. Only now did Shmoncel finally understand that his hands and feet were tickling Dodo to death. Her feathers were now all bristling. He quickly tried to get some down underneath him so that her crazy clip-clopping would not make him fall off.

Finally, Dodo was able to gasp for air. Her laughter stopped dead in its tracks and the familiar deep angry frown line appeared once more on her forehead. "Are you completely crazy? You know how ticklish I am. Why did you do that?" At that very moment, they heard some quiet sniggering. They both stopped short. "Was that you?" they asked each other at the same time. They looked at each other. There was no need to answer. "Hmm, I could have sworn that I just heard someone sniggering," whispered Dodo. They peered into the dark cave. "IS ANYBODY THHHEEERRREEEE?" bellowed Shmoncel as loud as he could into the cave.

At the very same moment Dodo leapt straight up. "Have you gone bananas?" she squawked. "I'm ringing down to my tail feathers! How can you just let loose like that right into my lughole?" "Well, if we're going into a cave like this one, the least we can do is ask if anyone's already in there." Shmoncel tried to change the subject. "It's as if we were ringing the doorbell ... " "But not my brain! I know that I'm here! Why do you have to ring on me like that? Do I have a doorbell for an ear?" Shmoncel crept back, receding under her feathers, accidentally tickling her again with his feet. The very next moment, Dodo was laughing and squawking and was off on her familiar tap dance. "Heaven help me!" called out poor Shmoncel. "Here we go again ... "

After a while, our two friends were able to think about exploring the cave again. Dodo decided that the sniggering was just something she had imagined. The pollen had probably made her groggy. "OK, I think we should just go in," said Dodo. "We can turn back any time we want." Shmoncel looked wary, but said nothing. All of his hands and feet were clinging to Dodo's feather coat. She squeezed herself between two thick branches. She had freed them of thorns, but the branches still wanted to block her entrance.

There was no stopping Dodo. She bulldozed her way through the obstacles. Now they were actually inside the entrance to the cave. "There we go!" she buzzed. "We must be the first ever to have set foot in here." "At least for a really long time," added Shmoncel. He now emerged a little from her feather coat. He was peeking around the cave in front of them.

They both felt a little creepy. After just a few steps, Shmoncel pleaded: "I think that's enough. We'd better go." "What? Hello!" protested Dodo.

"What's wrong with you now? We've only just made it inside and I'm now supposed to turn round? Am I crackers? Am I supposed to turn round now after all this work? You've got to make a better case than that, my dear!" But Shmoncel was not satisfied. Using all his powers of persuasion, he tried to stop Dodo from carrying on. "Utter nonsense!" Dodo put an end to the discussion. "I can do this with my left wing tied to my tail feathers." "Yes," grumbled Shmoncel, "while I fall off the other side. By the time we make it out, all the thorns and stuff will have grown back and I'll get skewered. Thorns are not exactly my cup of tea."

"Don't be such a chicken! You duck down, I'll get a good run-up and we'll get out easy-peasy." "Look, it's even growing into the darkness right back here. That's not normal!" Shmoncel carried on fussing. Three of his hands were pointing at the thorny branches that hugged the wall of the cave. Shmoncel burrowed down deeper into Dodo's feathers and held on tight. He closed his eyes and made his caterpillar body as small possible. Dodo went on, and as she did so she brushed against a small branch of the thorny bush which had grown deep into the cave. "OWWWWW!", cried Shmoncel. "OUCH! I've been skewered." Dodo looked at him. She saw right away that the tiny branch was merely touching his bristles. "What nonsense ... skewered ... Turn off your alarm, otherwise we won't get anywhere." "But, it skewered me ... "

"Nonsense," replied Dodo. "Maybe you got a little pinch. What's the problem? Pull yourself together and let's explore this cave! And stop bawling. My ears are still ringing from before." Shmoncel held on even tighter to Dodo's neck. He was very anxious about what might be waiting for them in there. Dodo gradually went further and further into the cave.

For all her bravado, Dodo was feeling uneasy. The roof of the cave was very jagged and spooky spikes hung all around them. The sun still shone weakly through the crevices in the roof just inside the cave. Dodo and Shmoncel opened their eyes wide, gradually getting used to their dim surroundings.

By now they could hardly see anything. Shmoncel was almost choking Dodo with his tiny hands pressing into her neck. Dodo was so tense she did not notice, but the gulping noises she was making, which were clearly audible, betrayed the fact that her throat had become a little tight. "Stay right there!" Shmoncel insisted. "I don't want to go into that darkness! We can't see a thing. Or are you going to try to make me believe that you can actually still see something in front of you? And what if somebody's dug a hole here in the path? We'd fall in and no one in the world would be able to save us. Stand still, I'm scared! You would suddenly fall in and you wouldn't see me any more. I would then be stuck here to slowly perish from lack of food and water ... !" "STOP IT!" screamed Dodo. "Don't panic! You're still up there on top of me." Dodo stood still. They looked into the darkness of the cave. Neither of them made a sound. "But if it makes you feel better," said Dodo whispering softly, "I can't actually go much further. I really can't see a thing. Wait a second — back there — there's something. There's something red back there, isn't there?" "Something dead?" replied Shmoncel aghast. He pressed his hands so hard into Dodo's neck that she croaked, started choking and gasped for air. "Oops," he mumbled letting go of her neck. Dodo audibly sucked in air. "Sorry! I think my hands have got cramp," whispered Shmoncel as he tenderly stroked her delicate neck feathers to try to make things better. "Something dead? — You don't seriously mean that, do you?!" he repeated peering wide-eyed past Dodo's neck into the darkness. "I said, something **RED**! With an R — **RRRRRRRR**."

Dodo rattled her beak which made an eerie, crackling echo. "AAAAAAAAAHHH, let's get out of here, Dodo, PLEASE!" begged Shmoncel. "I don't want to be in here. I'm a caterpillar. I belong in the sunlight." "You're my pal and you're staying right there on my back where you belong. Now stop panicking. I want to know what that red thing is. There's a red glow back there, don't you see?" Shmoncel was going to say that what she could see was only the red of her eyelids, but at that moment, he too could see a dark red glow not too far away on the cave wall ahead of them. Like an iridescent light floating faintly in the blackness. The cave wall came into view. It was glittering and moist. Slowly, Dodo inched her feet further and further forward. There was indeed a dark-red light glowing on the wall. "It looks wonderful," whispered Dodo. "What is it?" They could hear solitary drops of water dripping onto the ground. Earlier on they would have done anything just to have had a cool wet drink. Now they could not care less. "DRIP ... DROP ... DRIP ... " Apart from the water, there was an eerie silence in the cave, but even the silence seemed to have an echo. Dodo dared go no further. The constant drip-dropping of water, the echo and this red glow on the rock face captivated them both. Their mouths hung open in amazement. Shmoncel was again squeezing the air out of poor Dodo. Just as Dodo was about to complain, a ring of fire suddenly appeared in front of them and a large orange-red dragon bellowed "BE OFF WITH YOU — OR I WILL SCORCH YOU!" — as flames flickered from his mouth.

At first, Dodo and Shmoncel stood frozen on the spot. They did not flinch. Their eyes were as big as saucers. Neither did so much as wince, paralysed as they were with fear. In the first moments of shock, Shmoncel pulled Dodo's eyefeathers out to the side. 1 - 2 - 3 seconds passed by, and then suddenly they heard a snigger. A loud, hearty chuckle and the ring of fire disappeared. Instead of the large dragon, a mini dragon with teeny-weeny flames floated in the air before them. "Oops!" rattled the dragon. It was all too much for Dodo and Shmoncel. Dodo promptly did an about-turn and charged at full speed towards the exit of the cave, her little legs spinning in circles. She and Shmoncel were screaming their heads off.

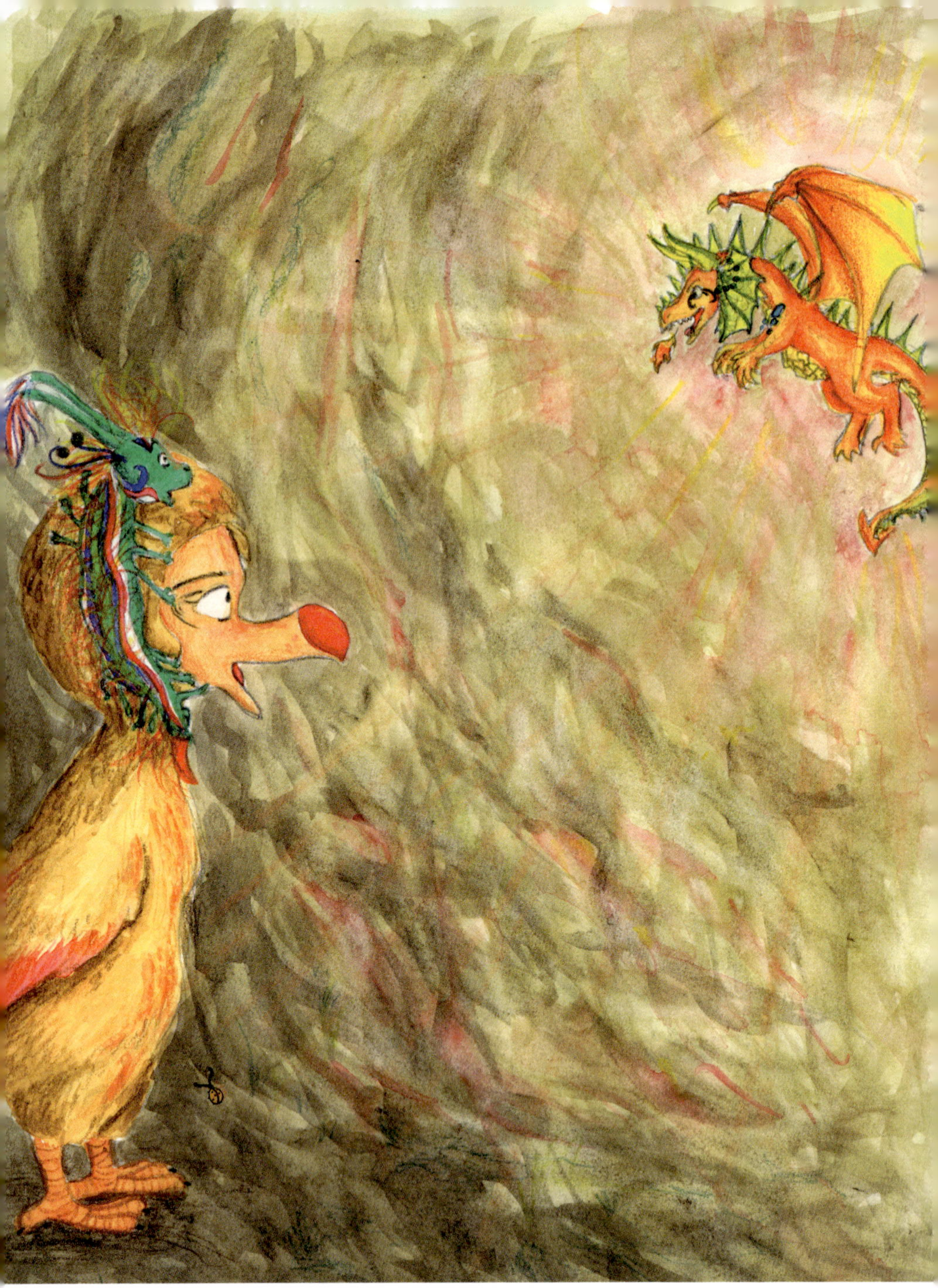

Shmoncel was still sitting on Dodo's back. Two pairs of feet were squeezing into Dodo's neck. His foremost pair of hands were pulling at her eye feathers like the reins of a horse. Dodo pulled her head in and opened her beak so wide that her lower jaw dropped right down to her chest and her upper jaw sat bolt upright. Her tiny uvula wobbled about as she squawked without taking a breath. Shmoncel yelled into her ear: "Shut your beak! I can't see a thing and you can't see where you're going!" Dodo, however, did not hear a word. She went on screaming. Her short legs carried on spinning as fast as they could. Her tail feathers stuck out straight behind her, standing out twice as wide as normal. Every single feather in her body stood on end. Shmoncel's bristles were also as stiff as a ramrod.

Dodo's little wings span madly like two propellers as if she had finally decided to learn to fly. From behind, she looked like three scoops of ice cream hopping around on an ice-cream cone trying to make a clumsy getaway. The echo in the cave turned the loud shrieking into a hellish and eerie din, which only made them both shriek even louder — if that were possible. Dodo and Shmoncel zoomed like a low-flying jet fighter towards the exit. When Dodo came to the front of the cave, Shmoncel screamed into her ear: "DUCK! Quick, I'm going to be spliced!" But Dodo was going much too fast. She made a beeline between the two branches, but in doing so she did not see the thick, thorny root which lay right in front of the cave. It had cruelly formed a little arch at that very spot.

Dodo's foot promptly caught on the root. She stumbled. A moment later she landed with a dull thud, sprawling on the ground and sending up a cloud of dust spiralling to the left, to the right and around her beak. This sudden braking and change of direction caused Shmoncel to catapult forwards and land like a spent arrow right in the middle of one of the big, beautiful purple-coloured orchid blossoms, which just happened to be by the entrance to the cave. There was a faint "Achooo" and the goblet-like calyx quivered wildly back and forth on its stem, as if it were a bell trying to sound an alarm. A huge cloud of orange-yellow pollen billowed out of the flower, expanding like a shimmering ball and giving off a sweet, vanilla-like fragrance. One half of Shmoncel hung in the flower. His other half dangled like a wet rag on a washing line. His little arms and legs oscillated limply back and forth in time with the swinging calyx. Dodo was out like a light. Her poor beak left a deep impression in the dust. As she came to, a bolt of pain shot through her entire body. It was as if each part of her body from beak to tailfeathers were reporting the fact nothing had been left in one piece.

n the midst of all this pain, Dodo suddenly heard gentle laughter. Gentle laughter, sniggering and something else. A constant "Hroff, Hroff, Hroff ... " Dodo slowly opened one eye. She then half-opened the other. Her foot then drew her attention in no uncertain way to the fact that it was still stuck underneath the root. Dodo let out a gentle groan: "Ow ... ow ... ow ... ow ... " She beheld the wobbling flower, half of Shmoncel and a bulging golden-coloured cloud. Then it dawned on her. Someone was laughing and giggling right behind her! She could now hear it loud and clear! "Rotten banana muncher. Who could be so mean?" was her next thought as the deep angry frown line again appeared on her forehead.

"**A**nyway," Dodo mused, "we still have a chance. We're not down and out yet. A giggling cave ghost can't be the devil." She slowly raised her head and turned it round.

A high-pitched little voice called out right behind her head: "Who are you?" Gentle sniggers. Dodo rolled her left eye further round towards where the voice had come from. There, floating over her, were a little fairy and a little red dragon! She was more than a bit spooked! The bright little voice piped up once again, "Can I help you? Where is your friend?" Only now did Dodo notice the "Hroff, Hruff ... cough, achoo, cough ... " coming from the orchid. The tiny fairy had noticed this too. She floated over to the large purple blossom, and took a magic wand out of her silky robes. Dodo was dumbfounded. She murmured quietly to herself, "I must be dreaming. This can't be true!"

Poor, unfortunate Shmoncel! He hung in the flower like a limp noodle and was in the middle of a protracted sneezing fit. Everything around him was covered in pollen. "Hroff, Hruff ... " On and on he went, blowing another huge cloud of pollen out of the opening of the flower like a pipesmoker blowing smoke rings into the air. "That's so cute," exclaimed the little fairy with the sweet little voice. Taking her magic wand she prodded it into the flower right onto Shmoncel's feelers. The fairy lifted the little chap, who was now sticking to the magic wand, out of the flower and set him carefully down next to Dodo. She was no bigger than Shmoncel himself!

Dodo stood, her beak half open once again, not knowing what to say, gawping in amazement and murmuring once more: "I have GOT to be dreaming. Can't be true ... Cannot be true ... " She had forgotten about the pain caused by her bent bones, and her battered rump. "Hroff, Hroff." The pollen spattered out in all directions, out of each and every bristle, ear, eye and nose. Shmoncel was oblivious to all of this. He was fighting for breath. Finally, Dodo pulled herself together and looked at the tiny being and the red dragon. Hesitantly she asked: "Who are YOU???" The sweet little voice responded gleefully: "I'm Sine, the Mountain Elf. And that's Fuzz, my fire-breathing dragon. And who are you?"

Finally, Shmoncel's pollen-sneezing concert came to an end. Imagine his amazement when he saw the two creatures floating before him. Dodo pulled in her little wings and tried to pull her legs together. After some laborious manoeuvres she sat up on her bottom and waggled her tailfeathers to give them a little more shape. She did not know whether to moan or marvel. She decided to marvel, throwing in the occasional "Ouch" whenever she moved one of her limbs. Shmoncel and Dodo kept staring wide-eyed and incredulous at the magical creatures before them. "You two are so cute!" gushed the fairy again. "Technically, we should chase you away, but you're just too cute ... You know, when I used my magic ring to make Fuzz look massive you two were so terribly frightened. Your eyes got sooo big!"

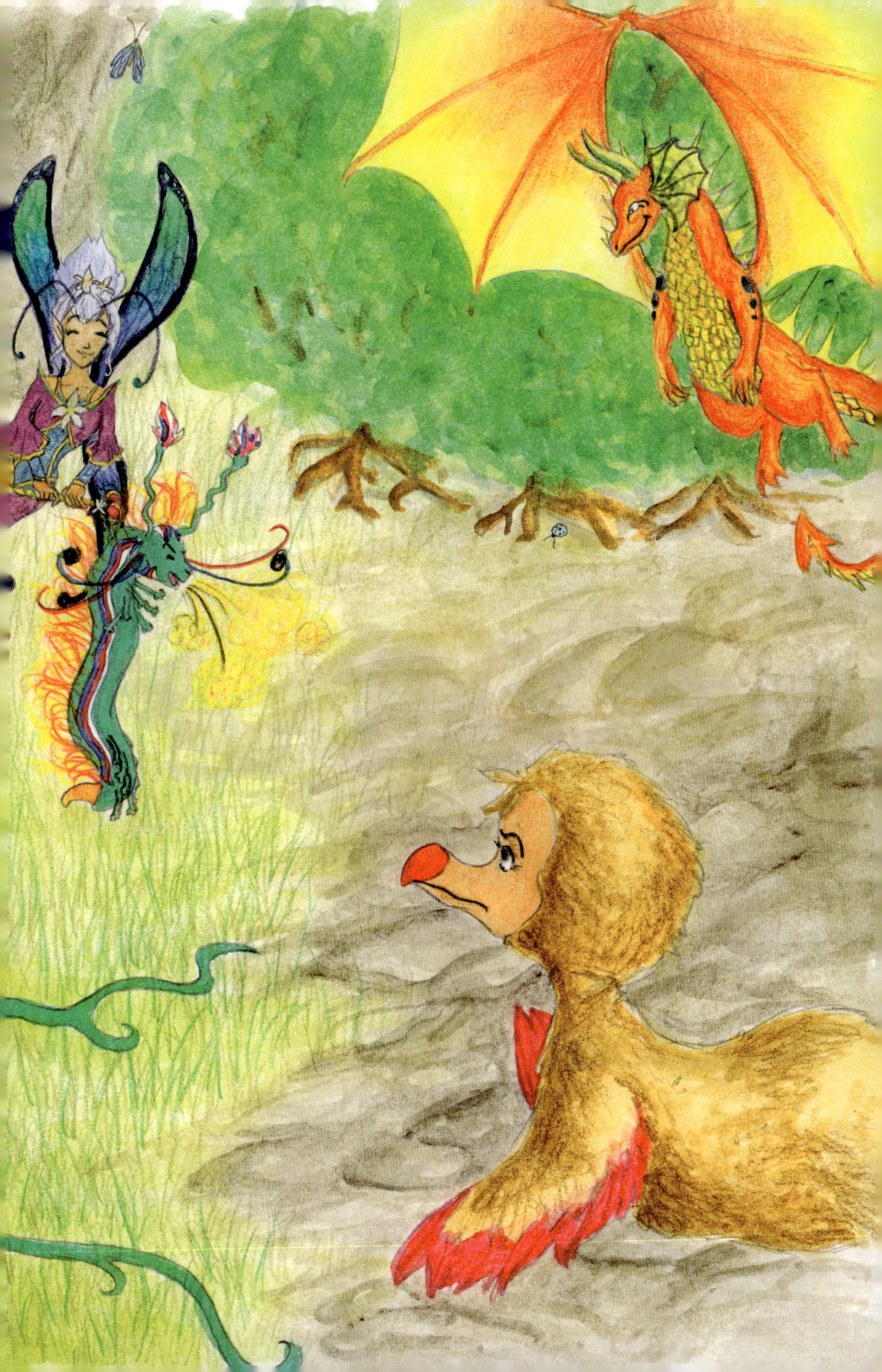

Sine spread her hands apart and used her magic wand to draw a circle in the air as big as a dinner plate. "Such huge eyes!" she repeated gleefully. "I just couldn't stop myself from laughing. That's why my magic can't work. Fuzz went back into his normal size. You looked sooooo cute and then you just took off. I couldn't take it anymore." With that, she started snorting with laughter again. Dodo's jaw fell open. At length Dodo asked again, with the same hesitation in her voice: "Tell me again who YOU are?" The sweet melodic voice twinkled once more: "You two must be really confused. I've introduced myself three times already. okay, I'm Sine, the Mountain Elf. I've lived an eternity in this cave. And that's Fuzz. My fire-breathing dragon. He's quite a small fire-breathing dragon, right Fuzz? That's why he's my type!" Sine and Fuzz smiled at each other. It looked as if they gave each other a slight bow. "He's always a great help to me in the cave with his shining coat of scales. Fuzz can make fire just like that, right Fuzz?!" Fuzz bowed again grinningd cheerfully. He growled. "Look at this ... PFFFFFUUUFF ... " he mumbled. Then he blew a fireball out in front of him. Dodo and Shmoncel's eyes were almost popping out of their heads. The fire had nearly singed their eyebrows. "Oh, sorry," growled Fuzz sheepishly, " ... I didn't mean to do that!" Dodo and Shmoncel were no longer frightened. They were now in a state of utter astonishment. In any case, poor Dodo was in so much pain nothing seemed to matter any more. Without moving a muscle, they let out a long drawn-out "Aaaaa-ha."

Sine again could not stop herself laughing. She collapsed in the air like a folding chair, slapped her knees and laughed so heartily with her bell-like voice that Fuzz could not stop giggling. He carefully held his little hands in front of his dragon snout to prevent the little flames from flickering out. "Those eyes, those eyes ... " Sine mused snorting with laughter again.

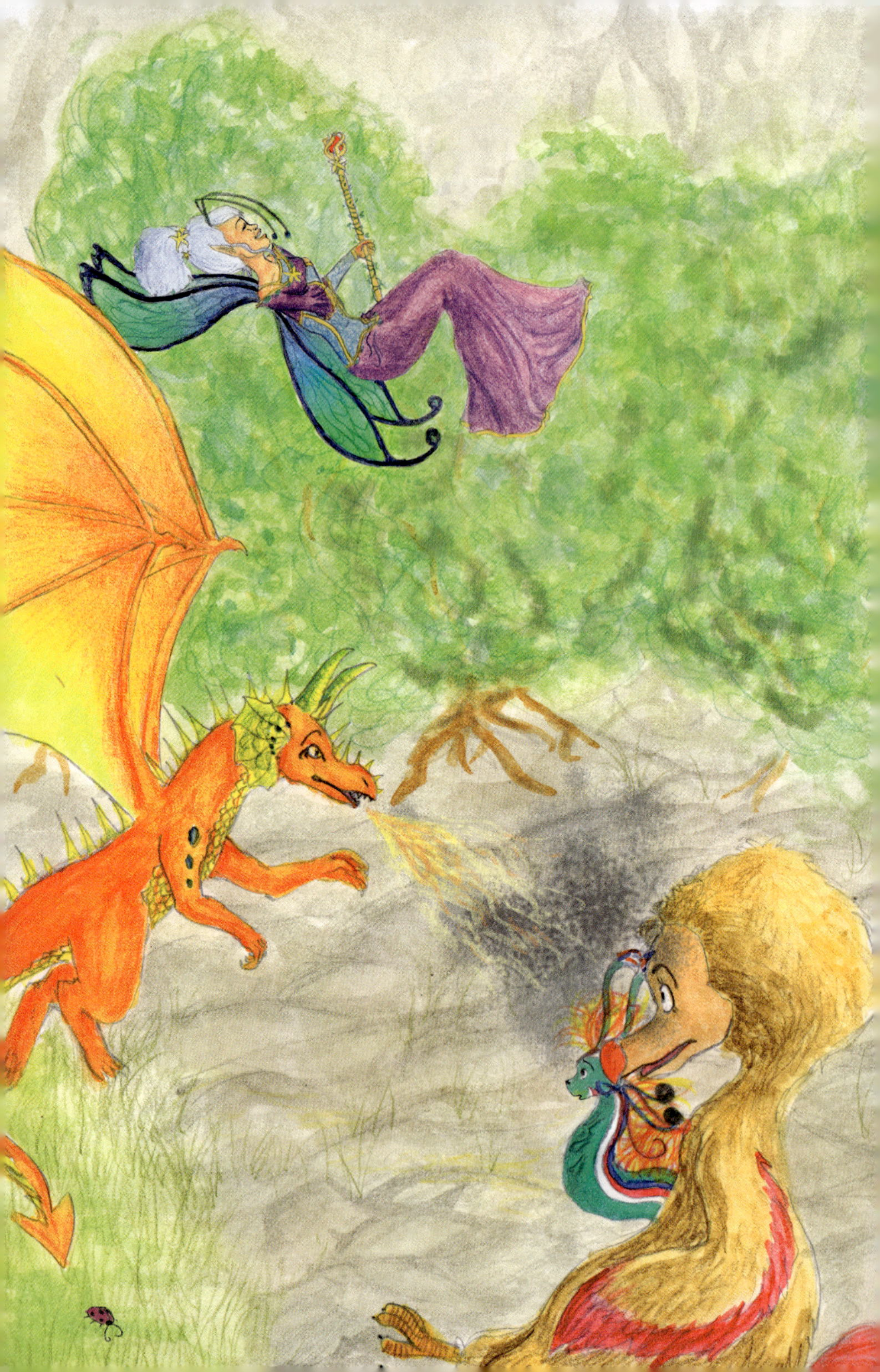

"You both have such wonderfully big eyes. Ah, if only I could see you both one more time ... But now, I have to go back inside to guard my treasure — but that's a big secret. I have got to look after it. Come on, Fuzz, we have to go. Not that anything else is going to happen. Now that would be a bad thing." Sine's little elf wings hummed in the air and she disappeared with Fuzz back into the cave, and as she did so she called back, giggling: "Call in again tomorrow, you two cuties! But you're not allowed to tell ANYONE. Never, ever. That's a promise!" The "That's a promise!" sounded as if Dodo and Shmoncel had already made a promise. It was forceful, more like a command. Any type of response was utterly pointless. Dodo and Shmoncel simply sat there and gawped like goldfish, open-beaked — excuse me, mouthed — as the two magical beings disappeared. Completely befuddled, the two friends flashed a questioning looked at each other and then peered at the entrance to the cave. "That was all a dream ... wasn't it?" stuttered Dodo quietly. "If it weren't for all this pain. My head, my legs, and especially my right foot. And my poor, poor tailfeathers. Not to mention my beak ... !" As she spoke, she carefully felt along her limbs until she got to her beak. She squinted at the tip of her beak, which she was feeling extra carefully. Shmoncel cleared his throat. It was dry and rough and in clearing it he sent out a few more little yellow clouds of pollen, which he tried to disperse by vigorously shaking his head and feelers. He finally took a deep breath of air and croaked at Dodo:

"I must admit that if I've had too much of my dad's honey wine, it explains everything, but ... Somehow I'm completely out of it. I'm not quite myself today. I can only remember us rushing out of the cave — and then everything goes blank ... Anyway, as far for your eyes, I have to say: You really do have very big eyes — you still do! Even though those two have already gone!" Dodo frowned. "You nincompoop! I wish I had seen your eyes ... But, come on, that can't have been real. We both dreamed up something which simply can't be true. Maybe the mangos didn't agree with us?" Suddenly Dodo pointed at the cave, wide-eyed: "There, look! The entrance! I tore a hole through the vines, but they're all overgrown and blossoming again ... just like before." "The smell's even stronger," said Shmoncel nonchalantly. It seemed as if nothing could rattle him any more. "It's just like a flower curtain on the front door. Probably the in-thing in these parts." He nodded and his feelers danced about wildly. At that moment they heard giggling and chuckling from the entrance to the cave. The soft echo made the giggling sound even stranger. Then came a clear sounding voice: "See you tomorrow!" Dodo and Shmoncel looked at each other again. "I've gone crazy," declared Shmoncel tersely.

"I now know that I am crazy. Let me climb up on your back, my legs can't carry me any more. We really have to go now. I just want to go home. I'll simply wake up, eat breakfast, and your Mama will tell me that it was only a dream ... " Dodo, meanwhile, was fingering her neck. "Strange, my throat feels as if someone has tied a cord around it and pulled. Really strange. It is as if it has been stuck down. Was that you?" Shmoncel was already sitting up on her back and was grinning like a Cheshire cat. "Perhaps I was a little afraid. When you have eight feet and six hands, as I do, things sometimes get a little mixed up, you know? I'm not used to such heroic feats from you. That was quite a show today!" "No kidding! That is probably the craziest thing I've ever experienced, and that's saying something!" declared Dodo, puffing herself out to the tips of her toenails and rotating her wings several times so that Shmoncel felt the whistling in his ears. Knowing what was coming, Shmoncel simply pulled his feelers out of the danger zone. "I think I need something to eat and drink right now. I'm kaput. But first of all, a bite to eat. I think I've just seen another mango." So began the long march home. No sooner had they started than Dodo started groaning about her ankle.

"Give me a break! I really didn't need that!" she gnarled angrily. She was forced to hobble a little. "I still don't get it," Shmoncel began. "The whole thing's crazy! We must have imagined it. It's just not on! A Mountain Elf! A fire-breathing dragon! Something like that in our day and age? It's not on! Somebody's trying to pull a fast one on us! — What I don't understand is: HOW?!?" "Yup," said Dodo drily, "... pulled a fast one on us ... whatever you say ... and my singed eyebrows, twisted beak, neck and ankle, and a pollen alcoholic floating through the air and landing right beside to me? You're spot on. It doesn't sound that convincing!"

"You're right," said Shmoncel, "but do you have ANY plausible explanation for what we just imagined back there? I don't." "I know that all this dreaming has knocked the stuffing out of me. I can feel it in my bones and it certainly feels very realistic. I feel a bit bent here and there, my dear! Not to mention the heart attack I suffered in the cave. Weak little dodo hearts are not cut out for such things. We put on a stunt show and our audience had a whale of a time. At least they got something out of it. By way of thanks they did not give us a grilling on this occasion. They just scared us to death for the fun of it. Even my eyelids feel worn out, as if there were bananas hanging from them ... " "I might just have an explanation ... " said Shmoncel. However, he then promptly took the view that it might not be such a good idea to tell Dodo why she was feeling so out of sorts.

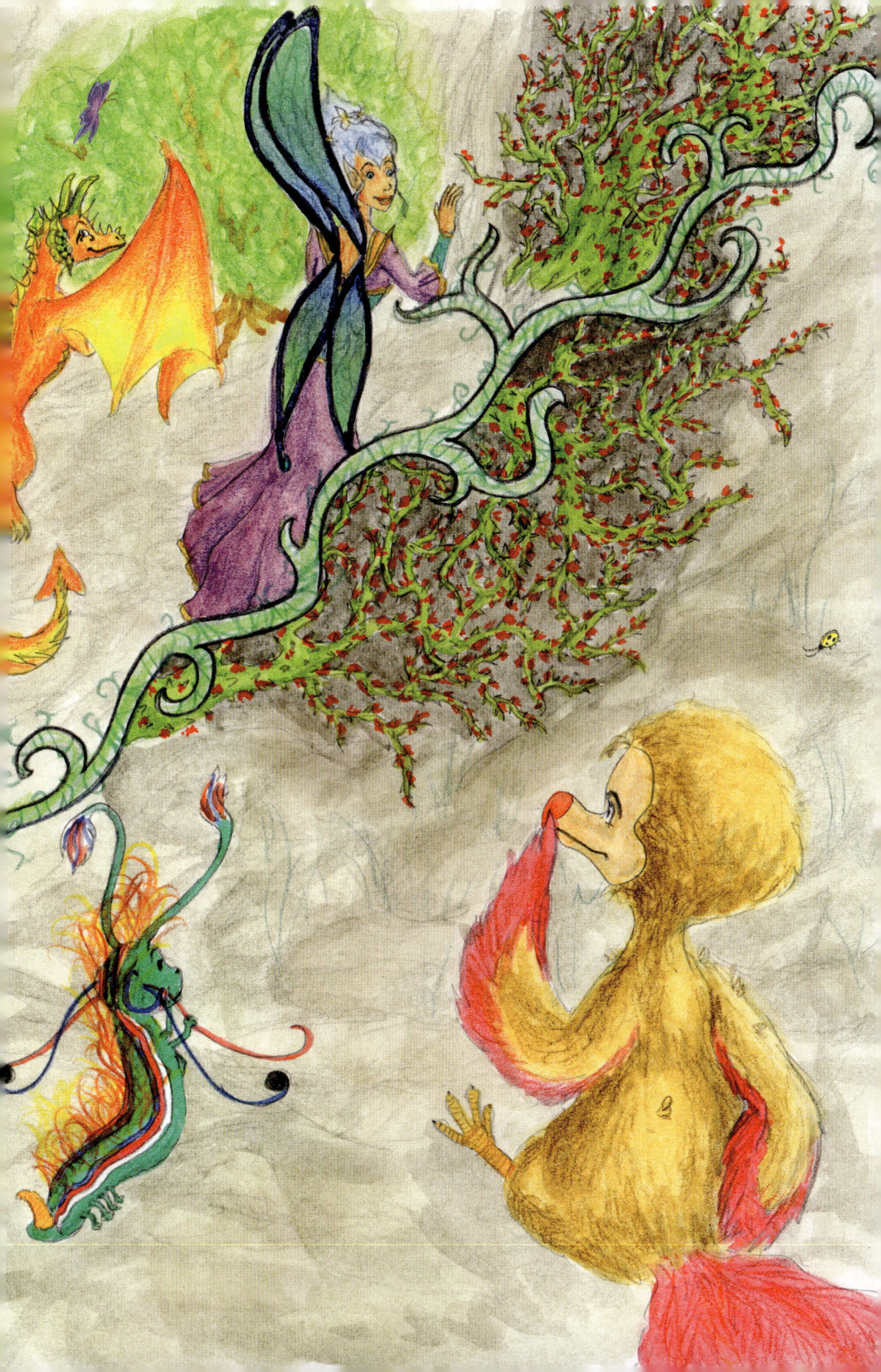

They kept turning round to look back at the entrance to the cave, which was now almost invisible behind the curtain of thorns. Thousands upon thousands of tiny blood-red flowers appeared to be waving goodbye to them in the gentle breeze. They let their gaze wander once more over the land and the sea and then looked down at the colony. This time they took it all in as if it were a dream. The day's events had left them in a daze. Eventually, they reached the edge of the rocky plateau, which they had climbed up earlier. Dodo was in two minds. "I'd love to go back there, go in again, and ask the elf … " she sighed dreamily.

"What do you want to ask? Ask if she's real? If I remember correctly, her name was Sine. Sounded something like "sign". I don't know if that's a good idea. Maybe she's changed her mind in the meantime, and she'll tell her flying blowtorch to flambé your tail-feathers as black as coal. I'm still totally exhausted. In my mind, I'm still running through the cave and I have the feeling that I can't move. Like in a horrible nightmare, you know?" "I have to say, you're absolutely right. Still, I would love to ask her, though I still can't believe it myself, whether we actually did experience all of that."

"Ahhh!" exclaimed Shmoncel, "Perhaps we got stung? Maybe a fat tsetse fly stung us, or the sun just cooked our brains. I don't know what to think. My mind tells me that it OUGHT not to have happened. And the longer I think about it, the less I seem to know. I see colourful pictures dancing before me. My brain is emptying faster and faster like a bucket of water with a hole that no one can stop. Presumably I won't know a thing soon, which would be no small wonder being a ... how did you put it ... oh yeah ... 'a pollen alcoholic'! Hopefully, I'll remember that one. It requires the right response at the right time ... " Shmoncel shook his head, his feelers dancing about wildly. "Now come on, Dodo," he droned, "We've really got to go home, as an E.T. would say. I wish I were already there. The sun is now too low for my liking. My appetite for adventure has been satisfied for today!"

t was a long way back, but they had so much to talk about and discuss. What kind of secret was the mountain elf talking about? In the valley, no one had ever said anything about mountain elves. They never wanted anyone to come up here alone because the mountain was bewitched. Yet no one had ever believed that ... What was this big secret they were on to? Why weren't they allowed to tell anyone about it? Right now all they wanted to do was to report back to the others as soon as possible to put everyone in the picture. They would then get the answers to all their questions. Papa Pushel knew everything. He always had a logical answer. They wanted to know what might happen if they talked about their experiences. After all, they preferred sharing exciting experiences and adventures and then telling others about them, discussing them and enjoying them together. Should all that be prohibited?

If only they had the chance to talk with somebody, at least to clear up the most important questions. How can you fumble about with a magic wand and then — just like that — send another one flying through the air? Shmoncel was greatly perturbed by this last thought! He could live to a ripe old age as a caterpillar, but still fly! "My goodness! If that were true, I could soon be flying!" Shmoncel was now suddenly dreaming out loud, rearing right up on Dodo's back. She winced: "Whoa, did you just scare me! Suddenly yelling out like that right behind me ... ! Don't expect too much from this flying! We dodos gave that up a long time ago. It's so much safer here on the ground. Anyway, your flight today wasn't exactly the bee's knees. Perhaps it was though ... bees love pollen — ha, ha, ha! I can still see your cloud of pollen in front of me ... pufff, pofff ... ha, ha, ha, ... !" "And I can still see your big eyes in front of me ... ha, ha, ha! ... " muttered Shmoncel, sounding a little insulted. They were both very tired. Slowly, they left the dense jungle behind them and entered forest which was far lighter. The path went steadily downhill. They made much better time than on the way up. Both were breathing heavily as they reached the flat open meadows near their home. They were almost there. It was high time. The sun was bidding a glorious farewell on the horizon in a magical shower of red shades. Inch by inch, the sun merged into the mighty forest behind the mountains. Step by step, Dodo steadfastly stomped on homeward-bound with Shmoncel on her back. The two would normally be rushing back in great excitement, but today they were reflective, deep in thought and — as I said — dead tired.

"Remember this morning? What a morning! We had such wild dreams! The flowers and blossom! And just a couple hours later, everything feels completely different, doesn't it?" Shmoncel nodded in agreement and his feelers danced ecstatically. And that was that. They went on their way without another word being said. They were just happy to have each other's company. Even when they were quiet and dwelling on their own thoughts, they could feel the other's warmth and proximity. They could sense what the other was thinking. Two close friends, who could count on each other and understand each other without anything said. Gradually, it dawned on them both that their Problem offered only one solution. Tomorrow, they would have to go back up to the plateau, come what may! There was a really big secret up there — and a really big adventure — which would eclipse everything they had been through so far. Today's adventure had surely been the biggest and most exciting of all their adventures. It was the greatest discovery Dodo and Shmoncel had ever made. By all appearances, there was even magic and sorcery at work too. They had a healthy respect for such forces. They were actually rather afraid after all they had been through. After all, they could have ended up in the soup — and they would have found the soup very hot indeed!

"**P**erfect weather!" said Dodo suddenly. "Imagine if the weather hadn't held out! It could easily have taken a turn for the worse ... " It was now Shmoncel's turn to wince and air his thoughts: "Yes, I was just thinking about how we would have fared up there if a real storm had blown up like the one we had last night. I don't even want to think about it."

In their own little world, they did not even notice Dodo's father waiting for them on the edge of the colony. He called out to them: "So, back home then?" Dodo looked at him with her big eyes and greeted him: "Hello daddio! It's great you're there! I'm really happy!" She spoke in a voice that sounded as if she would fall asleep on the spot. Shmoncel looked at him with a wide, but very peculiar, bleary-eyed grin. Papa raised one eyebrow. One gigantic eye was beaming down on them both. A dainty orchid blossom was hanging from his beak — the leftovers of the evening meal. It was on a long green stem.

Papa had planned to give them a stiff talking to punish them for their shenanigans. He had been so worried and frightened. However, now as he looked at them standing before him in their ramshackle state, he lowered his rump to half mast, heaved to, and took Dodo under his right wing. "Let's feed you up first of all. We were all worried sick about you two until Gigi suddenly told us that she had spotted you. You know jolly well that taking off like that without saying a word was not exactly a great idea. The Flattermann family is also in a flap. They couldn't find you anywhere, and they even flew up into the mountains to look for you. Hopefully, they'll be back soon."

Neither Dodo nor Shmoncel said a word. When Papa out of curiosity asked what they had been up to, back came the bland response, "That's a secret. I'm not meant to tell you. At least not yet." Papa scratched his ear. What was he supposed to glean from that? Something must have happened. Did the valley still hold secrets?

Could it be that they had gone up to the Mount Elfenberg, despite the fact that it was forbidden? But what kind of secrets could be up there? The elves had long gone. Papa looked this way and that and then back at his child. He looked thoughtfully at her friend and then back towards the mountain. He raised one eyebrow again and grumbled: "Well, we'll clear that up sometime. In any case, first comes dinner."

Gigi came running up and gave her sister a warm welcome, as she always did. With one big skip and a jump she was perched up on top of Shmoncel. Pinned down under Gigi's weight, the poor little fellow was helpless. He lolled out his tongue, his feelers stuck up like antennae, his eyes bulged as if they were about to burst, and his rump shot straight up in the air like a candle. Gigi squealed with joy! She grabbed on to the delicate feelers and rode poor Shmoncel like a cowboy. Dodo tried to stand with her legs apart and keep her balance, which had been seriously thrown off kilter by Gigi's wild cavorting. She was definitely back home!!!

Gigi was so overjoyed. Her sister was finally home again. Today, she did not even whine about riding poor Schmoz — which is what Gigi sometimes called him — as flat as a pancake. Shmoncel's tongue was dangling from the corner of his mouth and his eyes were squinting. He was begging for help and gasping for air. She kept holding on tight to the feelers and sat like a queen on her throne smiling triumphantly. Shmoncel looked like a slain dragon.

"Get down right now, you five ton sack of beans!" scolded Papa Pushel. He picked Gigi off Shmoncel as if she were a ripe berry. Shmoncel let out a long drawn-out "Pfffuuhhh ... !" and glanced gratefully at Papa. After wrenching and twisting his body back into shape, he grunted at Gigi:

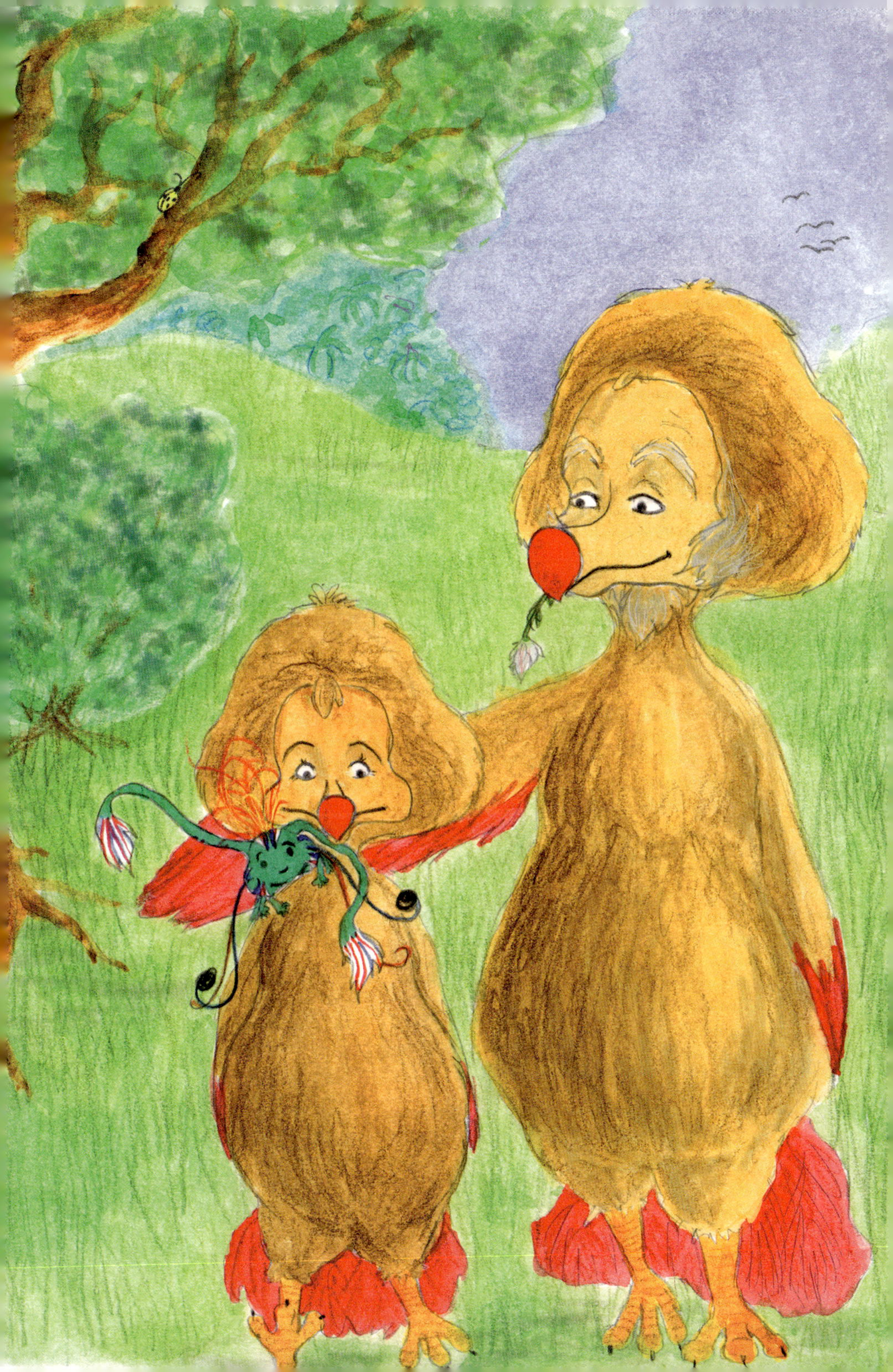

"That was some greeting, Gigi, but if you don't want me in a scrapbook, you shouldn't try to flatten me as if you were a coconut bomb! Anyway, it jeopardises my slim waistline. I could get rings on my belly and under my eyes. That just wouldn't be me." Gigi breezily brushed off his protests: "I love you all, my sweet little cuddlecakes!" Papa, Dodo, and Shmoncel could only shake their heads, a gesture to which Gigi paid not the slightest attention. She simply turned and marched ahead of them back to the colony.

That evening Dodo and Shmoncel snuggled down in the nest together. The dreamy-eyed friends had barely spoken over dinner, which was quite unlike them. Even Gigi's intrusive and annoying questions could not ruffle Dodo. "Yeah, yeah, that's still a secret," she kept repeating. That riled Gigi all the more. Finally, Mama took Gigi to one side and gave her a hug. "Give Dodo a bit of time," she whispered. "She's bound to have an incredibly exciting story to tell you once she's had time to think it over."

Right! Good point! Gigi turned her head, peered at Dodo, her eyes beaming and she gave a wide-beaked grin. "Really?" she asked. "You'll tell me the story then?" "Yeah, yeah," said Dodo, "but it's a big secret." "Oh, fine," crowed Gigi. "Then I'll be quiet now."

For the next ten minutes Gigi jabbered on about being absolutely quiet. She said that she would be as quiet as a mouse, that she would keep her beak as closed as a coconut — and that pigs would fly before she said another word. Everyone present could probably picture one or two of these images — and then hoped they would actually materialise ... Oh, dear Gigi!

By now there would normally have been a big bout of nagging and niggling between the older and the younger sister, but this evening there was nothing of the sort. Mama and Papa gave each other a quizzical look and shrugged their shoulders.

The whole affair remained a riddle. Nevertheless, they were sure that they would get more out of Dodo and Shmoncel the next day. Before the deep night sunk over the dodo colony and the moon bathed the peaceful hill in a silvery light, any neighbour that was curious and concerned had been notified that — well, how can I put it — the family actually knew nothing. This satisfied no one. However initial rumours of our two friends' terrifying adventure simmered in the background.

Little did they know that not even their worst fantasies could hold a candle to what Dodo and Shmoncel had actually experienced. In any case, Gigi was floating in seventh heaven. Tomorrow, she would find out a big secret! She could then go and tell all her friends ... and everyone would have to listen to her! That night Gigi slept with a satisfied grin on her beak. Her usual attempts at delaying bedtime for as long as possible just did not happen.

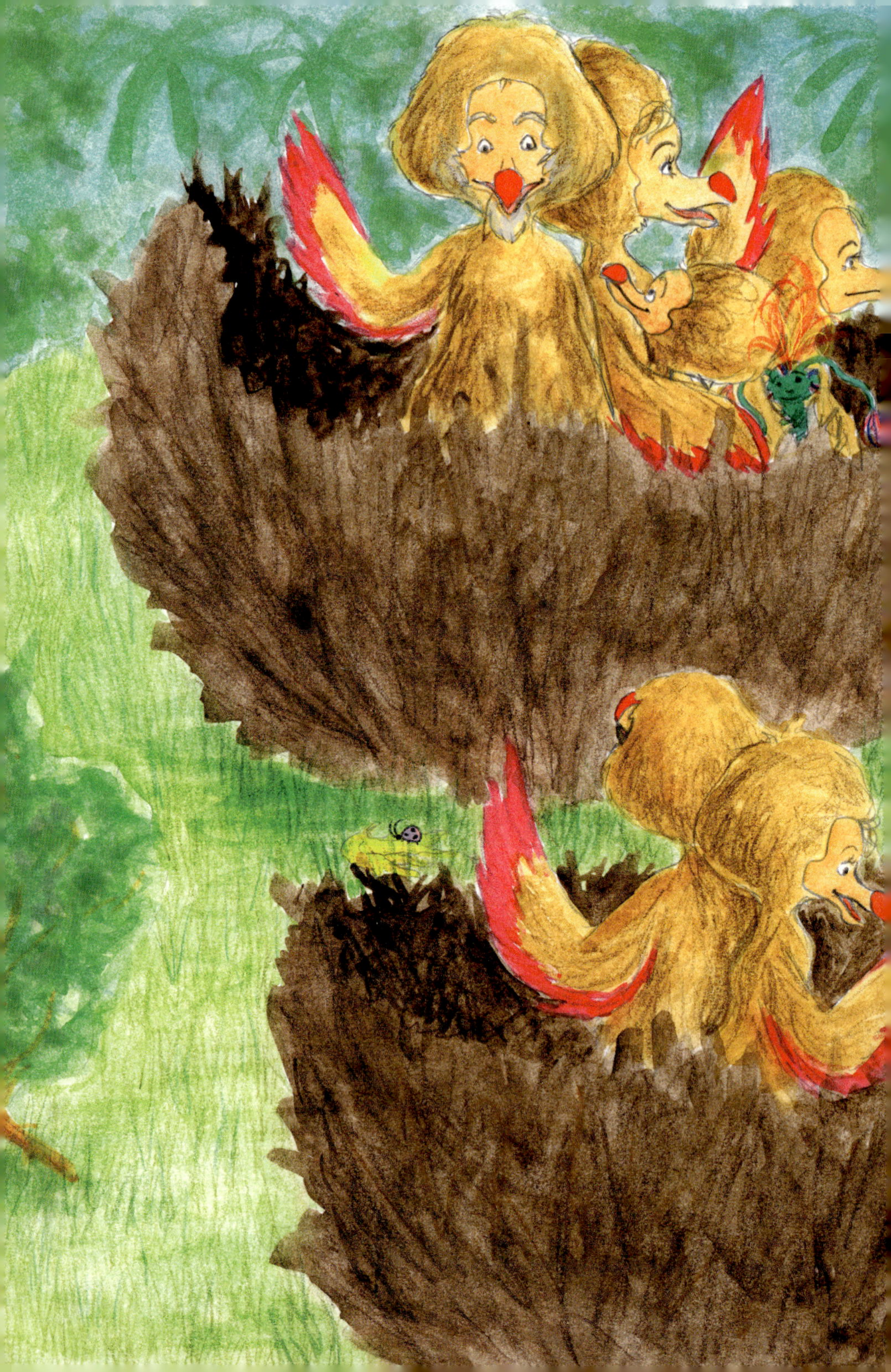

It was a starry night. There was not a single little cloud in the sky. The dodo families believed that this was a good omen. That night even the worst pessimists were sure that there was no need to worry about the weather. The Pushels were together again, and so too were the Flattermanns, who lived directly above the Pushels on the first Floor of the banana tree.

The stars twinkled up above and a warm breeze swept through the colony out towards the sea. The dodos began their "Good Night" chorus, which lasted for a full five minutes and ended in a confusing "G'NIIIIIGGGGHHHT", "G'NNNNNIGHT", "GOOOOOD NIGHT". This is what it meant to be a polite dodo! Finally, everything was peaceful and quiet. Only the soft roar of the surf could be heard in the distance and it lulled everyone to sleep. Almost everyone ...

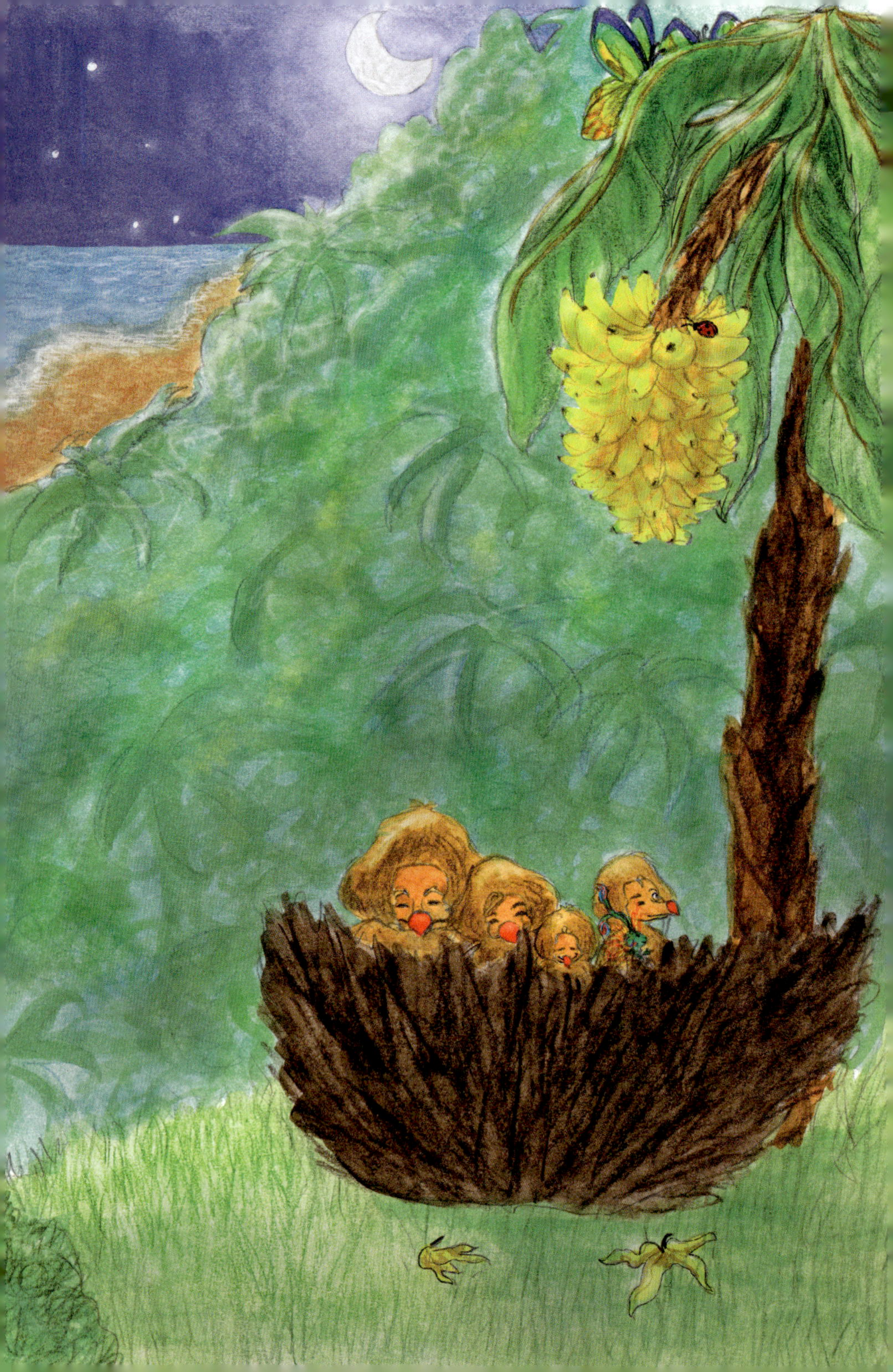

For a long time Dodo and Shmoncel looked towards the mountain with the jaguar head up on the rocky plateau. Their large eyes showed the reflection of the moon. They whispered softly to each tother: "We have to go back there tomorrow. We must find out what that secret is!" — and when they both claimed to have seen a red flash, their imagination stirred all the more. Fuzz? Had Fuzz wanted to send them a signal? It took them a very long time to fall asleep that night even though they were both dead tired. Hopefully the weather would hold out ... ?

Acknowledgements

A chain of events led to the creation of this little book. Many other people lent their help and support in order to turn it into a single unit. While the book was being produced the following people stood by me patiently in word and deed:

- My loving wife RITA, who was responsible for the digital production of capital letters, vines, beetles and snails. She did this with infinite patience.

- My dear daughter VERONIKA, who spent countless hours armed with brush and crayons and her unerring talent for drawing on the hunt for dodos. Veronika completed all the relevant illustrations with wit and humour in less than 4 months. She did not let the idiosyncrasies of watercolours, crayons and the author get to her — despite the pressures of high school and music school, preparing for her grade C organ examination, playing the organ in various churches, and taking her driver's licence! A real tour de force!

- My dear daughter REGINA, who used her imagination to help me turn the "little Christmas story" into the actual book. She was very understanding about the many hours when I was not able to play with her.

- My colleague S. MAYER who substituted for me in my real job and kept the office running while the boss went on dodo hunts and maintained his own dodo colony!

- The staff at Hinckel-Druck printers for providing excellent service!

- Edward DALE for his translation so close to the German text and Christopher HUMPHRIES for editing this flabbergasting story!

My sincerest thanks to all of you, especially Veronika, for your enormous support, without which this book would never have seen the light of day. What superb work! I look forward to more exciting collaboration in the next volume. It promises to be very exciting. The adventures can really take off now that we know the characters and their stomping grounds! Fuzz and the Mountain Elf are already waiting for us!

THOMAS STRUCHHOLZ
VEITSHÖCHHEIM, MARCH 2010

The Team of the Dodo Saga.

The Dodo family are also available as cuddlies. Please contact us to find out where you can find a retailer near you.
www.struchholzkunstgbr.de

Fuzz

Eines kleiner Feuerdrache

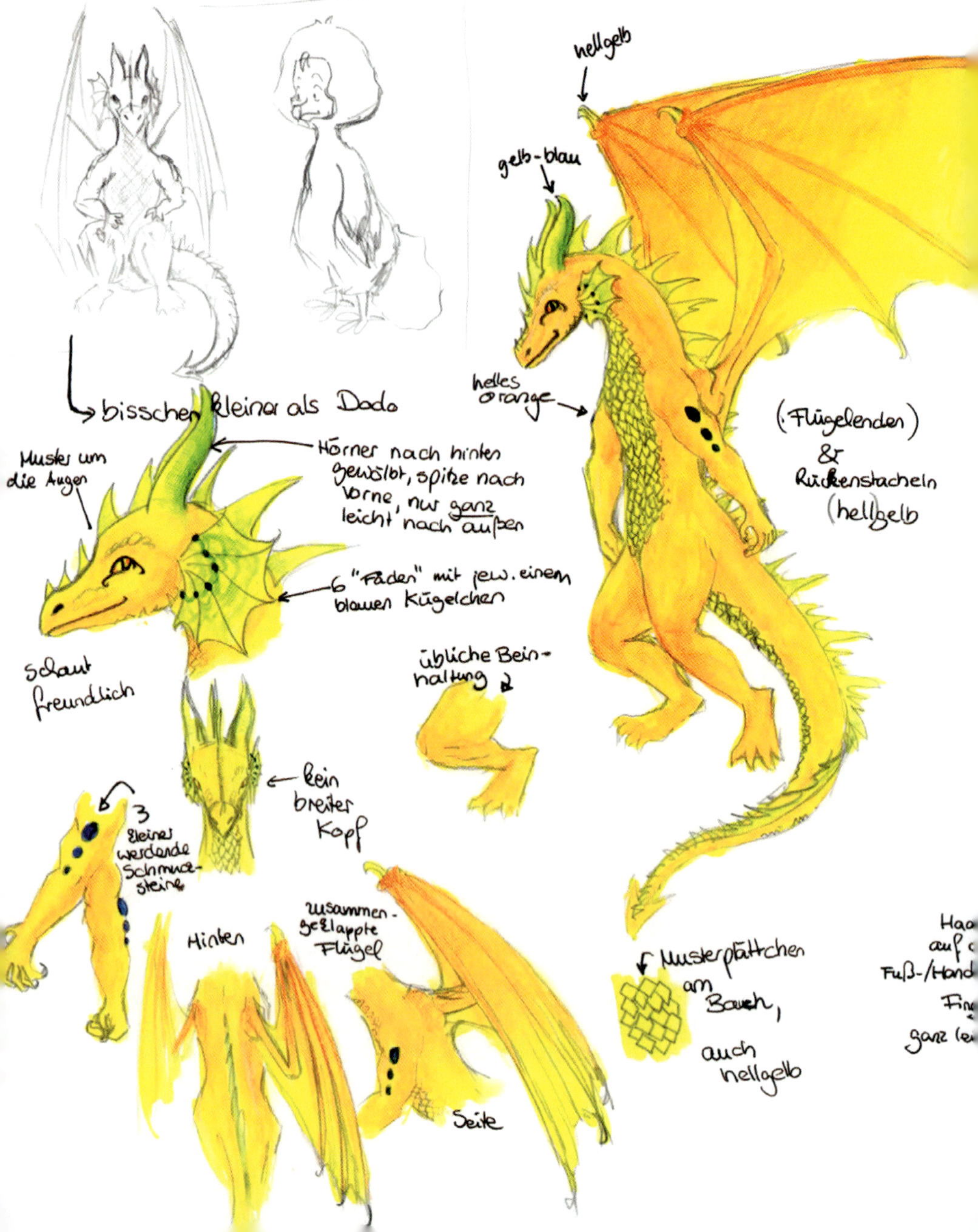

The work on the drawings took many hours and days including evenings, weekends - and a lot of free time! The cuddlies first had to be designed and then modified by paying close attention to the illustrations. Then Frau Hentschel's team at Sowema was able to turn this work into the finished product. The illustrator gave the fabric artist the most important details. On the left and above is an example of what a worksheet looks like!

Works published to date:

The Dodo Saga, Volume 1:
The Great Discovery
ISBN: 978-3-9812318-2-3

The Dodo Saga, Volume 2:
The Mountain Elf
ISBN: 978-3-9812318-3-0

Work in progress:

The Dodo Saga, Volume 3:
The Land of the Dragons

www.struchholzkunstgbr.de
mail@struchholzkunstgbr.de

Meer

Neriden Bucht

Hügel der Dronten

Jaguar

Plateau

zur Pfauen-Ebene ⇧   zu den Irrlichtebenen ⇧

Dschungel

Tal des Einhorns ➚

Yin-Wald

zur Grotte der Sphinx ➘

Berg-Wälder

zu den Vulkanen der Drachen ➘